A VINEYARD QUILT MYSTERY™

PATTERN OF BETRAYAL

MAE FOX &

Annie's

AnniesCraftStore.com

Library of Congress-in-Publication Data
Pattern of Betrayal / by Mae Fox & Amy Lillard
p. cm.
I. Title
                    2014916058

AnniesCraftStore.com
(800) 282-6643
A Vineyard Quilt Mystery™
Series Creator: Shari Lohner
Series Editors: Shari Lohner, Janice Tate, and Ken Tate
Cover Illustrator: Kelley McMorris

10 11 12 13 14 | Printed in USA | 9 8 7 6 5 4 3 2

PROLOGUE

"Set it on the desk and back away slowly." The mysterious figure known only as Ghost watched the cold surge of fear wash over the woman's face.

It was sad really. These museum security guards were just cop wannabes who had no idea of the true worth of the treasures they were supposed to keep safe.

The guard's eyes darted from Ghost's masked face to the gun pointed at her. She set the pre-Columbian statue on the desk and then raised her hands in the air as she backed away. "There. Please don't shoot me. I have a family, you know."

Yep. Ghost made it a point to know as much as he could about the people who guarded the priceless treasures he intended to take. He knew where they lived, what they drove, and where their kids went to school. He even knew what kind of ice cream they bought. "Just do as I say and no one has to get hurt. Understand?"

The guard nodded and backed up a couple more steps.

Ghost approached the desk and snatched the statue. It was about the size of a coffee can, a heavy thing, and ugly to boot. But it would fetch a fine price on the market. Ghost already had a buyer in mind. He tucked the statue under one arm, relishing the feel of it. *So much money.*

"You have what you came for," the guard said. "You should leave."

The woman seemed to be gaining back some of her moxie. But no matter. Ghost had the treasure.

"Your radio," Ghost said. "Put it on the desk."

She didn't move an inch.

"Radio. Desk. Now." Ghost set the statue down and leveled his gun at her.

She was at a distinct disadvantage. Pepper spray was the most dangerous thing on her utility belt. Still, Ghost didn't want a face full of capsaicin.

The guard pulled the device from her hip and laid it on the fine wooden desk.

"And your phone."

The guard looked as if she might protest, but she unclipped her phone and placed it next to her radio.

By the time he took the pepper spray, her hands were shaking.

Ghost slid the guard's phone across the desk and onto the floor, where he smashed it to bits with the heel of his shoe. The radio suffered the same fate.

The guard gasped. Judging by the look on her face, she feared her head would be next. But Ghost was a thief, not a killer.

Except for that one time ... but that was different. That guard had been mouthy, disrespectful, and had failed to follow instructions. As long as this one did as she was told, everything would be fine.

"I'm leaving now," Ghost said, scooping up the statue once more. "And you aren't to move until a full fifteen minutes have passed. I've got someone watching this building." It was a lie, but the guard didn't know that. "His instructions are to shoot anyone who tries to follow me, and then he'll go to 54 Carpenter Lane and shoot Sarah and Christopher while they eat their mint chocolate chip ice cream."

The woman choked back a cry; then she swallowed hard and nodded.

Ghost motioned with the gun. "On the floor. Now."

She looked almost relieved and did as instructed.

Good girl.

With a smile, Ghost strolled out the door, statue in one hand, gun in the other. It had gone well, but gloating would have to wait. A more pressing matter was at hand—getting from L.A. to Straussberg, Missouri, in time for the next job. Who would have thought a Victorian inn located in the middle of nowhere USA would be a lucrative target? Ghost sighed. In this business, one never knew where the next paycheck would come from. *Today it's a trendy museum ... tomorrow, the Quilt Haus Inn.*

ONE

"Salmon isn't going to be cost effective," Hannah Marks said. She adjusted her glasses and tapped the eraser end of her pencil against her notepad. "I decided to go with chicken. Joseph Winkler quoted me a good price on whole chickens from his organic farm. I figure coq au vin."

"Uh-huh." Julie Ellis stood at the front desk and ran her finger down the sign-in book for the Quilt Haus Inn. She pushed her dark hair over one shoulder and shook her head. "It's crazy."

"Coq au vin is French, but I wouldn't say it's crazy." Hannah looked up from her notepad. "Have you heard a word I've said?"

"Sorry," Julie said, her steady gaze transfixed on the open book in front of her. "We had a cancellation yesterday, but it looks like we're booked solid now." Which was a good thing since this would be the first ever Quilt Haus Inn murder mystery weekend. How Julie had ever allowed the newly retired owner, Millie Rogers, to talk her into holding the event she'd never know. Murder was one thing she had seen more than enough of lately.

"Yep," Hannah said. "I booked the last room."

"When?" Julie looked up at her good friend and assistant, the painfully level-headed woman who had followed her from the big city to a touristy village in Missouri to live the quiet life. It was an unexpected yet necessary move after Julie had unwittingly angered a few of the wrong people in her former profession as an antiquities recovery expert. But Hannah seemed to really enjoy the slower pace of small-town living. Julie was … learning to adjust.

Hannah shrugged. "I booked it late yesterday afternoon."

"But it was cancelled late yesterday afternoon. I took the call myself."

"Consider it a blessing."

Julie would consider it something, though she wasn't sure blessing was the right word. Strange coincidence, maybe.

Until that point, she had been struggling to book rooms for Millie's experimental murder mystery weekend—an idea the owner had hatched as she was making plans to retire and get to work on her bucket list. Then Millie had "skedaddled" off to see the cave paintings of Baja and left Julie to figure out how to make it work. In order to get the reservations needed for the unique weekend event, Julie had been forced to go outside their normal venues. After all, their target guest list was even more specialized than usual. They normally catered primarily to quilters and seamsters. For this event, they were seeking the same people, but ones who were also murder mystery buffs.

In Julie's opinion, they should have waited until autumn to host the event so they'd have a full year to plan instead of only a few months. But once Millie set her mind to something, it was hard to move her from it. So, they advertised and posted the upcoming fun to the inn's website and everywhere else Julie could think of. Even with the ad in the number four mystery magazine in the country, it was only at the last minute that the rooms had filled up. Just last week they had had only two confirmed reservations. A short five days later they were full.

"So, what do you think?" Hannah asked.

"I think it's strange."

"You think chicken is strange?"

"I'm sorry ... what?"

Hannah closed her notepad. "I knew you weren't listening to me."

Julie smiled at her sheepishly. Ever since they'd arrived in Straussberg, a small tourist destination in the rolling hills of Missouri wine country, Hannah had taken her job as head cook at the Quilt Haus Inn *very* seriously.

"You're right. I wasn't," Julie said. "And I apologize. But I know whatever you serve will be amazing."

Hannah blew out a frustrated breath, stirring the blond hair that had escaped her ponytail. "I've just never served a dinner before. I mean, not here. And I want it to be perfect."

"It will be."

Shirley Ott poked her head around the corner, her bright red hair like a copper halo. "It's showtime!" she singsonged. She looked particularly festive in her grass-green skirt and bright yellow gypsy top. The scarf looped around her neck was patterned with every color of flower known to man and then some. Shirley was the resident storyteller and keeper of the small fabric shop and tearoom on the first floor of the inn. She loved all things bright and colorful, even in her hair, and sewed most of her clothes herself. "I thought you'd want to know that the first few guests have arrived. They're in the tearoom." With a wink, she turned and disappeared, a blur of red, yellow, and green.

"And so it begins." Julie began heading out to greet her guests, pausing to glance back at Hannah. "Are you coming?"

Her friend shook her head. "I'll meet everyone soon enough. I really need to get dinner started." Hannah gave Julie a tight-lipped smile and hurried toward the kitchen.

"Don't fret," Julie called after her. "You can't go wrong with coq au vin."

Hannah stopped and gave her friend a genuine smile, and then headed into the kitchen, shaking her head.

In appearance, the inn was as charming as a bed-and-breakfast could be. Victorian-era furniture and matching accessories filled the large mansion, with special attention given to the popular gathering area of the tearoom/fabric shop, which was run by Shirley. The main level also boasted a cozy library, a formal dining room, and a large breakfast room with white-linen–covered tables.

Julie still felt somewhat uneasy about the last-minute bookings, and she nearly sighed with relief when she saw the two little elderly women sitting in the tearoom, sipping from their cups and enjoying the latest treat from Hannah's kitchen. They looked normal enough. *Why am I being so paranoid about this?*

"Ladies," Julie said in greeting as she entered the room. "I'm Julie Ellis, your innkeeper. I'd like to welcome you to the Quilt Haus Inn."

The ladies nodded in unison. They both wore polyester pantsuits in bright colors with cream-color shells underneath.

"I'm Sadie Davidson," the thinner of the two women said. Her suit was a bright aqua and made Julie think of the swimming pools in Miami. Three strands of perfectly matched aqua-color beads hung around Sadie's neck and clacked together as she moved. "And this is my bestie, Joyce Fillmore."

Bestie? Julie figured at least one of these two ladies had granddaughters. "It's so good to have you both here." She offered a welcoming smile.

Joyce smiled in return. Unlike Sadie, who had snow white hair, Joyce seemed to favor a blue rinse that made her own cap of curls shine like periwinkle chrome. She was tall and solid, a handsome woman.

"We are so happy to be here!" Joyce exclaimed. "This was on our bucket list."

"A murder mystery weekend was on your bucket list?" Julie asked.

"Number twenty-five," Joyce said. "This inn is the *perfect* place ..." Joyce turned to Sadie and added dramatically, "for someone to die."

Julie laughed with Sadie. She was starting to think this wasn't such a bad idea.

"An inn with a quilting theme is an added bonus, to be sure." Sadie smiled, revealing twin dimples in her rosy cheeks. She looked like the quintessential granny, a large purse with a twist clasp looped over one arm. Julie suspected her big white suitcase likely contained everything from peppermints and tissues to bingo daubers and an extra tube of nude lipstick.

Julie went on to explain the amenities of the Quilt Haus Inn, particularly those that catered to quilters and crafters. "This weekend we have an Amish-style quilting frolic to go along with the murder mystery."

The quilt frolic had been Hannah's idea, a way to bring Millie's murder mystery brainchild to life and still keep some kind of quilting theme.

"Tell us, dear," Sadie asked, "how will it work?"

"Yes. When will someone die?" Joyce added. They'd clearly been "besties" for a long time.

Julie smiled. "It's simple, really. We'll have special meeting times throughout the day so everyone can get together to quilt and discuss the clues in the case as things unfold. At the end of the weekend, the quilt will be given to the guest who solves the case."

"And the winner also gets a free weekend stay next year, right, dear?" Sadie pressed.

"That's right." Julie nodded as the sound of a voice outside caught her attention. "Ladies, it's been a pleasure.

Please enjoy your tea. I'll check you in at the front desk when you're finished."

The ladies gave another synchronized nod, and Julie left the tearoom.

The bell above the door chimed. The couple that strode into the foyer consisted of a bored-looking man with thinning brown hair and a small frown, and a woman who looked happy enough for the both of them. The man's attire seemed somewhat out of place for mid-Missouri—khaki shorts, athletic sandals, and a Hawaiian print shirt that was loud and untucked. Julie got the feeling he'd rather be anyplace else in the world. It was as if he'd planned to vacation in an exotic locale and somehow ended up in Straussberg instead.

"Hi," the woman gushed, removing her floppy white hat. She pushed her sunglasses onto the top of her head to perch like a plastic tiara on her frizzy hair. "We're the Calhouns. Susan and Kenneth." She pointed at herself and her husband in turn, as if Julie wouldn't be able to figure out who was who without a little help.

"Welcome," Julie said with a smile. She introduced herself as they registered and took their key. "Everyone is gathering in the tearoom before the event starts. If you'd like to get settled first—"

"Oh, no," Susan said with a wave of her hand. "We can do that later."

"I'll show you the way, then," Julie said as she helped Kenneth settle their bags by the front desk.

Julie led them to the tearoom where she hoped some refreshments and a story or two from Shirley would make Kenneth look a little less like he'd rather be having dental work done. Julie got the distinct impression that the whole weekend had been Susan's idea. Julie hoped he would reign in his less-than-enthusiastic attitude and play his part in the mystery like a good sport.

For the next hour and a half, Julie checked in guests, handed out keys, and directed the motley group of mystery quilters to the tearoom. Aside from Sadie, Joyce, Susan, and Kenneth, the guest list included Alice Peyton, a fifty-something divorcée whose frown was deeper and wider than Kenneth's. Alice told them all that she had received the trip as a gift from her kids, but she didn't look very happy about it. Maybe, like Kenneth, she'd had her sights set on someplace with a beach.

Dr. Liam Preston also joined the group. He was handsome in a bookish sort of way, with wire-rimmed glasses, wavy blond hair, and a dimpled chin. He introduced himself as a professor of literary studies. He certainly looked the part with his khaki trousers and tweed blazer complete with leather patches at the elbows. What he *didn't* look like was a quilter. But Julie kept her mouth shut. She'd learned the hard way with a previous guest, Daniel Franklin, that looks could be deceiving.

Julie had been more than a little caught off guard last autumn when the ruggedly handsome Daniel had stepped into the lobby and requested a room. She hadn't pegged him for the type to enjoy something as quiet and traditionally feminine as quilting. Yet, he knew more than most about patterns and techniques. He'd decided to remain in Straussberg and open a museum. Now he was something of a friend—a very handsome friend. But that wasn't the point. No, the point was that she vowed not to make assumptions about any of her guests again.

She tried to apply that same theory to Gregory Wilson, the forty-year-old bachelor standing across the room from her. Gregory had a thinning patch of light hair, a middle-aged paunch, and beady eyes that shone behind thick glasses. He made no effort to share his motivation for attending the weekend event. In fact, he didn't say much at all. He simply listened to everyone tell their stories while he drank his tea in silence. Suspicious silence.

"I'm not going to judge," Julie whispered to herself as she waited for the last guest. "I am *not* going to judge."

Carrie Windsor, the first guest to make a reservation and the last one to arrive, finally skittered into the inn a half hour before the festivities were set to begin. Like Gregory, she wore glasses. Unlike Gregory, her oversized specs ate up half of her petite face, covering it from forehead to cheeks. She wore her pale blond hair pulled back with a claw clip, a few tendrils escaping to wisp around her face like a shaggy halo. The youngest in the group, she appeared to be no more than eighteen. Yet her eyes, though covered by the glasses, had an age about them that belied her pixie stature and innocent air. She looked a little like she had been caught in a storm, her clothes windblown and stretched out. In fact, everything she wore looked faded and old, as if she'd owned it since the dawn of time. She smiled politely and ducked her head as Julie handed her a room key.

Once Carrie was checked in, Julie joined the guests in the tearoom as they listened to Shirley spin her latest tale. *What a group.* She had a feeling the weekend would be anything but boring.

Shirley was clearly enjoying it. She nearly beamed with joy at having such a captive audience. She'd been telling stories for so long, her voice had started to turn hoarse, and she was drinking almost as much tea as she served. As she finished a tale about the ghost who reportedly lived at a local farm and occasionally killed the chickens, Julie made her way to the front of the group.

Hiding a smile, Julie refrained from pointing out that it might have been a fox doing the dirty deed. Better to let Shirley have her fun.

"That's all well and good, dear," Sadie said to Shirley, "but what I *really* want to hear about is the Civil War journal you found here."

A murmur of agreement rippled among the guests.

"You found a Civil War journal?" Liam Preston asked mid-sip. The tiny floral-patterned teacup he held looked ridiculous in his large hands.

"It's not a journal per se," Julie interjected. "More of a manual that someone wrote in. But the entries date back to 1861."

"What a treasure!" Liam exclaimed. "Wherever did you find it?"

"In the basement," Julie said. "I was looking through some old boxes and happened upon it." She didn't add that she was trying to find an item for an upcoming school auction at the time. She switched her focus to Sadie. "How did you know about the book?"

"There was an article in the local paper about it, dear," Sadie said.

Julie regarded her curiously. There *had* been an article in the local paper, but that didn't explain how Sadie knew about it. She wasn't from Straussberg.

"The article was picked up by a couple of larger papers," Joyce added, as if reading her mind. "I read about it in the *Danville Times*. That's our paper."

"And then there's the article on the Internet," Sadie continued. "That's how I heard about it."

The Internet? Julie thought Sadie might pull a smartphone out of her handbag and show her the story.

She found it hard to believe anyone would give much

thought to the old manual. When she'd first discovered it, she called an expert in Civil War memorabilia and told him what she'd found. He'd asked her several questions about the book and then had her take some digital photographs of the pages and send them to him. An hour later he'd called back to say it wasn't worth more than two or three hundred dollars—to the right buyer. Julie thought that was perfect for the auction, though she still hadn't received approval from Millie to donate it to the local school.

Clearly the inn's feisty owner had better things to do in Baja than answer emails as Julie still hadn't received a response to her question about the book. Though annoyed by the delay, Julie knew that she'd be hard-pressed to answer her email, too, if she had the choice between looking at prehistoric paintings or a laptop.

"Will you show us the book?" Carrie asked timidly. "It sounds fascinating."

Julie studied her for a moment. It was the first time the young girl had spoken since they'd entered the tearoom.

"Yes," Liam added, "I would love to take a peek at it."

Of course he would, Julie thought. He was a professor of literature.

She gazed around at the eager faces. Well, *most* of the faces were eager. Sadie, Joyce, and Susan Calhoun looked as interested as Liam and Carrie, while Kenneth Calhoun, Alice Peyton, and Gregory Wilson ranged from bored to indifferent.

Julie checked her watch. She was going to break in a few minutes so her guests would have enough time to settle in and get ready for the next event. "I suppose I could show it to you."

A chorus of yays rose from some of the guests, and Julie went to her office to retrieve the book. She had locked it inside the inn's safe, more out of habit than true worry about the book being stolen. With deft fingers, she maneuvered the combination lock and extracted the manual.

She hadn't taken the time to read everything in it, handwritten or otherwise, but she could tell from the worn leather cover that it was very old. She'd done a little research online but wasn't able to contact more than the one expert before she'd been forced to shift her focus back to planning the weekend's activities.

"Here it is," Julie said as she returned to the tearoom. The guests crowded around to look at the tiny bound book.

"That is truly spectacular," Liam said. He cupped one palm under his chin. Julie thought all he needed was a pipe to complete his professorial look, or maybe a smoking jacket and crackling fire. But the late-spring Missouri weather was much too warm for a fire.

After a few minutes of the guests oohing and aahing over the old relic, Julie checked her watch. "Ladies and gentlemen, I believe it's time to get this mystery weekend under way. You should have received your character sketches in the mail a few weeks ago. A big thank-you goes out to Shirley for creating such entertaining characters and such a shrewd killer." The guests all clapped, and Shirley gave a quick curtsy.

"Just to refresh everyone's memory," Julie continued, "this will mostly be an off-the-cuff event. It's not a play. Your names and relationships have not been changed for the event, though your histories and backgrounds have been rewritten. This is not a team event, so even if you are here as a pair ..." She looked from Sadie and Joyce to the Calhouns. "... it's every player for himself."

Joyce clasped her hands. "Oh, this is so exciting!"

Julie chuckled. "We've got forty-five minutes before dinner.

So, please settle in and change into whatever costumes you brought and get into character. Remember, the success of this event rides on your shoulders. The more participation we have from you, the better experience everyone will have. Any questions?"

Sadie raised her hand. "Will we be able to finish our dinner? I have to take medication at mealtimes, and if I don't eat enough I tend to get ..." She blushed. "Well, it's not good, dear."

Julie smiled indulgently at the woman. "I can't tell you when the murder will take place, but I will personally see to it that you have plenty to eat."

"Thank you, dear."

"Anyone else?"

The guests shifted anxiously and shook their heads. The enthusiastic faces had turned eager, and the bored ones still appeared ... well, bored. Julie couldn't help but wonder why someone would commit to such an event if they weren't at all interested.

The guests filed out of the tearoom, and she watched them go. Kenneth's attitude she could almost understand; it was obvious he'd come because his wife wanted to attend. But Alice and Gregory were something of a mystery.

Shirley rubbed her hands together, her round face lighting up with excitement. "This is going to be so much fun. We should think about holding a murder mystery event at least twice a year."

"Let's wait and see if we survive this one first," Julie said.

"Hello?" A male voice called from the foyer.

"That must be Brandon," Shirley said, referring to the actor they had hired to play a key role in the mystery.

"Good. Have you seen Daniel yet today?" Julie asked

Shirley as they made their way to the front of the inn.

"Right here." Daniel's tall frame stood in the foyer next to the young actor.

Both men were dressed in costume. Since Brandon was a member of the local community theater, his costume was detailed and spot-on. He had the perfect turn-of-the-century cut to his coat and waistcoat.

Julie couldn't quite pin down the exact era of Daniel's ensemble. Not because she didn't know period dress, but because his interpretation of late-1800s fashion looked a bit more ... eclectic than those seen in a museum.

Regardless, he still managed to look rugged and handsome. But Julie knew better than to get involved with men like him. She'd been down that road before. She *would* ignore the playful twinkle in his eyes and the way his white shirt made him appear even tanner. He was a stuffy old treasure hunter. Why couldn't he just look like one?

"I really appreciate you helping us tonight," she told the pair.

"It's my pleasure." Daniel smiled, revealing deep dimples and even, white teeth.

"Glad to help," Brandon said, casting a sidelong glance at Shirley. "I am still getting paid, right?"

Julie shot Shirley a look.

The redhead simply nodded. "Fifty dollars."

"Cool," he said. "Thanks, Aunt Shirley."

"I'll show you where you need to be." Shirley took his arm and led her nephew toward the dining room.

"And to think, you got me for free," Daniel said, giving Julie another one of his killer smiles.

"You're not my nephew."

Daniel's eyes darkened. "No, I'm not."

Something in his tone sent little shivers down her spine.

Focus, Julie. She eyed his puffy shirt and riding pants. A pirate. That was what he reminded her of. A turn-of-the-century pirate. She raised an eyebrow and didn't even try to hide her smile.

"What?" Daniel asked with a laugh. "You don't like my costume?"

"Riding pants?"

"It was the best I could do. I don't have the resources of Straussberg's community theater wardrobe department at my disposal."

"I suppose not." Julie looped her arm through one of his and led him out of the foyer. "Come along, Captain Jack. I'll show you what you're supposed to do. Then I've got to run upstairs and change."

"If you need any costuming advice—"

"Oh, does your pirate tailor work this late?" Julie asked, looking at her watch.

"I hope so. I forgot my eye patch."

TWO

Surprisingly, it turned out that Daniel's costume was actually one of the better ones among the group gathered in the dining room.

Kenneth, in keeping with his previous bored attitude, had donned a George Washington–style coat over his Hawaiian print shirt. He'd at least changed out of his khaki shorts and put on khaki *slacks*. If Julie had been handing out prizes for the worst-dressed, he would have won hands down.

On the other end of the spectrum was Gregory. He looked like a character straight out of an Edith Wharton novel—authentic and impeccable. Everyone else fell somewhere in between.

Sadie and Joyce had traded their pantsuits for dresses reminiscent of Little Bo Peep's. All they needed to complete their looks were shepherd's hooks. Both dresses were blue, but Joyce's was just enough on the aqua side that it spectacularly clashed with her hair.

"Oh, look at that dress!" Sadie exclaimed as Julie entered the room. "Almost as glamorous as the one Scarlett wore."

"Scarlett O'Hara?" Julie asked, glancing down at her dress. It was dark purple, not red, and not nearly as revealing as the one from *Gone with the Wind*. She gave the bodice a little tug just to be on the safe side.

"No, silly," Joyce said. "Scarlett Jones."

Julie blinked. "Who's Scarlett Jones?"

"A good friend of ours," Sadie said with an impatient sigh. Then she took a long sip of wine, as if Julie should've known which Scarlett they were referring to.

Julie could only smile in response.

The two women bustled off to comment on Susan's dress, their petticoats rustling as they moved. Like Gregory, Susan had gone all out, wearing long white gloves and a sparkling bracelet glittering around one wrist. She looked cool and sophisticated in emerald green.

"There you are!" Shirley exclaimed as tiny Carrie Windsor entered the room, a timid expression on her face. Wrapped in a pastel pink sateen dress with big puffy sleeves, a heart-shaped bodice, and a drop waist, Carrie looked like she was headed for her high school prom ... in 1987. Her glasses still dominated her face, though she had managed to secure all of her hair in some sort of French twist. She looked wholly uncomfortable as Shirley dove in for a hug.

Inga Mehl, the inn's housekeeper, marched into the room wearing her usual frown and drab gray dress. She was something of a fixture at the inn, having worked there for many years. No-nonsense, highly efficient, and stealthy, Inga still carried a slight accent from her native Germany and insisted on wearing the staid gray uniform of a traditional domestic while at work, even though Millie didn't require it. Though she was a part of the murder mystery, she'd refused to wear a costume, forcing Shirley to rewrite her part so that she could "play" the part of a housekeeper.

And then there was Alice, the spitting image of a prairie woman from the late 1800s. Her dress was high-necked, long-sleeved, and made from a pale yellow calico. Although her costume was sorely out of date, she blended right in with the rest of the diverse group. It wasn't exactly how Julie had pictured the party, but it was the spirit of the thing that mattered.

Julie stood at the head of the dinner table and clinked a spoon against her wine glass. "Good evening, everyone," she said as the chatter died down. "As you all know, tonight *someone* will be murdered." She paused for drama, looking at each guest in turn.

"Until then," Julie continued, "enjoy your meal and get to know one another. And stay in character as much as possible. This is a chance to just have fun being someone else for a couple of days."

"Here, here!" Susan shouted.

Everyone raised their glasses in a toast.

Julie sat back in her seat as Hannah emerged from the kitchen with a rolling cart of food and numerous bread baskets. Everyone got the same meal, which was plated in the kitchen and served efficiently with Inga's help.

Soon, all that could be heard was the clanking of silverware and the murmur of conversation as the guests warmed up to playing their parts in the mystery.

"Good idea to have dinner first," Daniel said, leaning close to Julie.

She nodded. "This way everyone will have time to get used to their characters before the mystery actually begins."

Daniel smiled and gave her a wink. "No, because I'm starving."

She shot him an exasperated look. He merely widened his smile and then took a bite of his bread.

It really was a shame he was so handsome. Maybe in another life, at another time, she could have fallen for him. But right now? She was a little tied up, hiding out from international art thieves. She and Hannah had come to Straussberg for one purpose and one purpose only: to save their bacon. Yet, somehow in the process, she had gotten entrenched in being Julie Ellis, a humble inn manager. And she actually rather enjoyed it.

Daniel caught her eye again and pointed to his watch.

She knew what he was silently asking, *How long until it's time to start the show?* Julie glanced at the large grandfather clock on the other side of the room. It was seven fifteen. Shortly before eight, the lights would flicker and then go out. When they came back on, the "body" would be found, and the mystery would begin.

She leaned closer to him. "Quit worrying about the time, and get your part done. You need to start planting clues."

He nodded and then turned in his seat toward the other guests. "I say," he began in what had to be the worst British accent Julie had ever heard, not to mention overly loud. "You look a tad familiar, old chap. Have we met?"

The other guests swiveled their attention to Daniel as they tried to figure out who he was talking to.

Brandon looked up from his chicken and glanced around the table as if to check and see if Daniel was really talking to him.

Julie had to admit, the kid was pretty good.

On cue, Shirley ducked her head in shame. She let out a gusty sigh, dragging everyone's attention from Brandon to her.

Everything was going as planned.

"I don't think so, sir," young Brandon replied. "I'm new to these parts."

"I see." Daniel sat back in his seat, his eyes narrowed in dramatic fashion.

A long pause followed. The next line was supposed to be Inga's, but she was having trouble getting into the swing of the evening. It would have been better for everyone if Julie had been successful in luring Hannah out of the kitchen to play Inga's part, but Hannah had stated quite emphatically that she would quit on the spot if they did anything other than ask her to serve dessert. Poor, stoic Inga had been brought on instead. And she was already failing miserably.

Shirley nudged Inga with one shoulder, somehow making it seem like an accident.

"Oh." Inga turned a bright shade of red. "Uh. What about you? I don't remember seeing you around much." She recited her lines in her usual deadpan monotone.

Daniel adopted a cool air, like a riverboat gambler holding four aces. "My wife and I like to travel. We've been through here many times. Haven't we, dearest?"

Shirley beamed at him. "Oh, yes, and we just love staying at the Quilt Haus Inn whenever we're in the area." Shirley's animated performance was as over the top as Inga's was below it.

"Indeed we do." Daniel smiled at Julie, who was playing the part of the innkeeper—big stretch—and then shifted his attention back to Brandon. "But I can't shake the feeling that I've seen you somewhere before. On the riverboat, perhaps?"

Brandon shivered. "No sir, I get sick as a dog on the water. No sir, that wasn't me on the riverboat."

Julie checked the clock. Seven thirty. They still had half an hour of playacting and banter before the lights were scheduled to go off. So far, so good.

The thought had no sooner crossed her mind than the lights flickered and went out.

Knowing they were in the midst of a murder mystery dinner, it should have taken no one by surprise when the room went dark—surely not enough that they would scream.

But someone did.

Chills ran down Julie's spine. The lights weren't supposed to go out so early. But there must have been a simple explanation for it. Hannah probably got the "kill time" mixed up.

Any minute now, she would flip the lights back on, and the mystery would begin. There was no need for alarm.

But the lights didn't come back on.

"What's going on here?" It was a male voice, and Julie thought it sounded like Liam.

"Julie?" This from Shirley.

"Are the lights supposed to stay out this long?" Joyce asked.

"I would have thought they'd be back on by now." This came from Sadie.

"Hannah," Julie called.

"What happened?" Hannah replied from the dark kitchen doorway.

"You didn't do this then?" Julie asked.

"Definitely not."

"You must have blown a fuse or tripped a breaker," Daniel said.

Julie carefully stood, keeping her hands on the table. "OK everyone, we seem to be experiencing a technical difficulty. I apologize for the delay. Please remain in your seats while Daniel and I check the breaker box. Hopefully we'll have the lights back on in a jiff." Though she wasn't sure how she was going to accomplish that. The place was nearly pitch black. How was she going to find her way to the breaker box? "Hannah, could you light the candles in here?"

"I'm on it," Hannah said.

"Oh my, I think something just brushed my back." Joyce said. "What in the world—"

A stifled sigh was heard, followed by a muffled thump.

"What was *that*?" Susan asked.

Julie wasn't about to say it sounded a lot like a body hitting the floor. In the dark, it could have been anything. Her imagination was getting out of hand.

"I'm sure it was nothing." Julie did her best to keep her voice calm.

"Everyone stay put," Daniel said.

Julie felt his hand at the small of her back and wondered how he could even find her in the dark room. But she was thankful he did. After all of her exploits chasing treasures through the dark streets of foreign countries … well, it was one thing to be in the dark by choice and quite another to have that rug of comfort pulled from beneath your feet.

"I think there's a flashlight in the foyer desk," she said as he steered them toward the exit.

"Here we go." Daniel led the way through the dining room doors and toward the front of the inn. A dim light shone in through the front windows, offering them a fighting chance of finding the flashlight.

Julie rummaged through the desk, which was a little more cluttered than she remembered. The bulk of the desk cast thick shadows onto the contents of the drawers, making it that much harder to find what she was looking for. Her fingers finally felt the cold, round, metal object they were searching for.

"Got it," she said triumphantly. She held it above her head in victory; then she lowered it, switched it on, and silently thanked whatever kind soul had last put in the batteries. The beam of light was strong and true.

"To the breaker box," she said.

"Any idea where it is?"

"Yes. Follow me." Relocating the breaker box was one of the first things she'd done when she had taken over. "It's in the second-floor linen closet."

"The linen closet?" Even with only the glow of a flashlight beam reflecting on his face, Julie could tell Daniel was frowning.

She shrugged. "I had it moved from the basement in case we ever have an issue with floodwaters." She started toward the stairs.

"Floodwaters?"

"Hey, you can never be too careful."

Daniel followed her up to the second floor. "I suppose not."

"Unless you're Hannah," Julie added.

Daniel laughed as they made their way down the hall to the linen closet.

Julie opened the door and peered inside. "Here, hold this." She handed the flashlight to Daniel, moved a stack of towels to the side, and opened the door to the breaker box.

"They all look OK," Daniel said, shining the light inside.

"Looks can be deceiving." Julie methodically began flipping each switch one way and then the other.

Daniel shook his head. "That wouldn't be the problem. The entire inn is without power. Each one of those would only control a room or two. You need the main switch."

Julie squinted at the tabs. "Which one of these is the main one?"

He studied the switches and then shook his head. "None of them."

Julie wiggled out from between the closet and him. "How's that?"

"The main switch doesn't have to be in the same box with the others. In fact, it can be on a completely different floor."

"How do you know so much about this?"

Daniel shrugged nonchalantly, but she could tell he was pleased with her backhanded compliment. "I had an uncle who was an electrician."

"Your uncle wouldn't happen to know where the main switch would be, would he?"

"No. But if I had to guess, I would say it's somewhere near the kitchen."

"Oh, yeah?"

Again he shrugged. "It seems like a good place to put it in case of a fire. In fact, it may have been moved there for that very purpose. I'm surprised the electrician didn't mention this when he moved the box."

"Me too." Julie smiled in admiration. "Lead the way, detective."

This time she followed Daniel as he led her back downstairs. After searching the entire kitchen and the surrounding area, they finally located the main switch in the tearoom. Julie thought it was strange that she had never noticed it before. Oh, she had seen it, but had never given the small metal plate on the wall a second thought.

Daniel opened the door and peered inside. "See, there's the problem." He wiggled the breaker to show the play and then snapped it back in place. After moving two more switches back and forth, the inn was flooded with light.

No sooner had Julie blinked everything into focus than another scream pierced the night.

"Oh no," she said and raced toward the dining room with Daniel close on her heels. Julie hadn't realized just how big the inn really was until she was running through it, summoned by a shriek.

"Oh my, oh my, oh my, ...," someone said over and over again.

"That sounds like Susan," Julie said as she and Daniel skidded around the corner and into the dining room.

"Do something," Inga demanded of Julie.

Julie looked down to where the grim housekeeper's calloused finger was pointing and saw the body of Alice Peyton sprawled out on the floor. A dark spot stained the floor near her head, and a heavy brass candlestick lay off to one side.

"Julie?" Shirley asked, a slight tremble in her voice. "I don't understand. This wasn't—"

"I'm calling an ambulance," Inga said.

Dear God, please let Alice be alive, Julie silently beseeched, gently falling to her knees beside the body. Was this the source of the thump they'd heard earlier?

Hesitantly, Julie reached out two fingers and lightly touched the woman's throat.

No pulse.

Maybe I'm not doing it right. Julie moved her fingers a little to the right, then a little to the left. Still nothing.

Her eyes met Daniel's as he knelt beside her. He lifted Alice's limp hand and pressed his fingers to her wrist. After a few seconds, he shook his head.

"Well?" Shirley demanded as Daniel pushed to his feet.

Julie slowly stood. Another murder; it was only a few months ago that Daniel's best friend, George Benning, had been murdered. This time, it was blatantly obvious that this was murder.

"*Well?*" Shirley asked again. Her tone more of a shriek this time.

Julie shook her head.

Finally, Daniel broke the tense silence. "She's dead."

THREE

"But she's *supposed* to be dead, isn't she?" Susan asked. She stood off to one side with Kenneth hovering slightly in front of her as if he were protecting her from everyone else in the room.

"Of course she is," Sadie said. "Alice is our murder victim. Isn't that right, Julie dear?"

"I didn't think any of the guests were supposed to be the victim," Joyce interjected.

"We don't need an ambulance," Julie murmured, still shocked by the grim turn of events. "We need to call the police." She looked at Daniel to find he already had his cell-phone pressed to his ear.

"Yes," Daniel said into the phone. "The Quilt Haus Inn. Thank you." He tapped his phone off. "Done," he said to Julie.

"The police?" Susan asked, the weight of the situation finally settling in.

"I knew I felt something brush behind my back in the dark," Joyce said. She looked accusingly at Carrie. "It felt like something short and small."

Carrie let out a small gasp as all eyes in the room swung in her direction, her face turning bright crimson. "It wasn't me!"

"Well, I'm certain I heard footsteps near my chair right after the lights went out," Gregory said. "They were heavy footsteps. Like that of a man." He eyed the other men in the room with suspicion, casting a brief glance at Inga too.

"This is absurd," Liam said. "I'm not going to stand around in a room with a dead body and a room full of suspects listening while we all accuse each other of murder."

Julie turned to Shirley. "Why don't you take everyone into the tearoom? I think it would be best if the guests remain together—and out of this room."

Shirley swallowed hard and then nodded.

The guests cast accusatory looks at one another as Shirley, with a little help from Inga, herded them out of the dining room. Only Brandon, Daniel, and Julie remained.

"Brandon?" Julie turned toward the young actor. He stared at the body with disbelieving eyes. "Brandon?" she said, louder this time.

"Huh?" He jerked his gaze up to meet Julie's.

"Perhaps you should join the others in the tearoom."

His wide-eyed gaze strayed to the body and then quickly back to Julie. "Yeah, I think I will." He hustled out of the room as if someone had set fire to his feet, leaving Julie and Daniel alone with Alice's body.

Julie sighed. "Now I guess we wait?"

Daniel nodded. "But I don't think we should wait in here. It's probably best if we join the others in the tearoom—if for no other reason than to keep a war from breaking out."

Julie slowly nodded, although joining the others was the last thing she wanted to do. Or was it that she didn't want to leave the body of Alice sprawled out on the dining room floor? It seemed wrong somehow to simply walk away when someone had just suffered such a wicked end.

"And you're sure she's …?" Julie waved a hand around, reluctant to say the word.

"Unfortunately, yes."

Julie gave a stiff nod. "I guess I'd better go tell Hannah. I'm not sure she has any idea what's really going on in here."

"I'll go check on the others."

Julie managed a small smile. "Thank you, Daniel. I'm so glad you're here."

He looked to the body on the floor and then back up to Julie's eyes. "Me too." He sighed, giving Julie a wan smile, and then headed toward the tearoom.

Julie couldn't stop her gaze from darting back to Alice one more time. She tried to remember what she had learned about the woman from their earlier conversations. Alice was fifty-something with a couple of grown children, recently divorced, and a bit bitter about it if the downward curve of her mouth was any indication. That was about all Julie knew.

"Oh my stars!"

Julie whirled around as Hannah walked into the room carrying two large pillar candles and a box of matches.

"What happened in here?" Hannah asked as she dumped the candles onto the table.

Julie shook her head. "I'm not sure. But Alice is ... dead."

"But she wasn't even supposed to be the victim." Hannah searched Julie's face as if waiting for her friend to laugh and say it was all a joke.

"No," Julie said simply. "She wasn't."

A noise sounded from the foyer.

"The police must be here," Julie said. With any luck it wouldn't be the same officer who had investigated George Benning's murder last fall. Julie had seen enough of Detective Everett Frost to last a lifetime. "Stay close by," Julie said to Hannah. "I'm sure they'll want to speak to everyone, whether you were in the room when it happened or not."

Hannah nodded, cast one last look at poor Alice, and then scuttled to the kitchen as fast as she could go.

Julie left the dining room just in time to see her "favorite" detective duck into the tearoom.

Fabulous, she thought wryly.

Two more uniformed officers and a paramedic rounded the corner and walked toward her.

"Is this where she is?" the paramedic asked.

Julie nodded mutely.

They pushed into the dining room, and the paramedic knelt beside Alice. He felt the pulse points. "No vitals," he said. "I'll call it in. We're either going to have to transport her or wait for the coroner to make the official call."

One of the officers nodded and then headed toward the tearoom. Julie followed close behind. When she entered the room, she met the shocked expressions of her guests.

The weekend was *not* going at all as planned.

The officer joined Detective Frost and said something quietly to him that made the detective nod. Then the officer left the room again.

"You don't understand. She wasn't supposed to die," Shirley blurted. She appeared to be on the brink of tears.

Julie cringed as Detective Frost turned his hawklike stare from Shirley to her. "Hello, detective."

"Julie Ellis," he greeted. "Why am I not surprised to find you in the middle of all this?"

Before Julie could reply, Susan asked, "If she wasn't supposed to die, who was?" The woman's nose was red, a telltale sign she'd been crying. Her husband had one arm wrapped protectively around her, even though his eyes sparkled with interest.

"What do you mean?" Frost demanded. "Was this a murder gone wrong?"

"We had a murder mystery event planned for this weekend," Julie said. "There was supposed to be a *fake* murder, part of the act."

"I was the one who was to die," Inga said stiffly as she

stepped forward. A few people started at her words, as if they hadn't realized she was there until she spoke. Julie could sympathize. Inga had the same effect on her.

"Well, settle in, folks, because no one's going anywhere until I get some statements." Detective Frost pinned them each with one of his cold stares. "From what we can tell, someone was murdered here tonight, and it's my job to get to the bottom of it."

Julie sighed. It was going to be one long night.

Thankfully, two more detectives arrived to help take witness statements. One was talking to Susan and Kenneth while Sadie and Joyce sat down with the other. Liam, Gregory, and Carrie sat at a table with Shirley and drank coffee. Everyone was obviously shaken.

It was just Julie's luck that Detective Frost was the lead on the case. Naturally, he wanted to talk to her personally.

"Now, tell me how this all came to be," he said to Julie.

She ran through the highlights: Millie wanted them to host a murder mystery weekend, and today was the first day of the event. Alice was a guest at the inn. Julie didn't know who would want to kill her or why. She didn't know anything about her other than what they had talked about in the tearoom. Everything at dinner had been in character.

"And the … uh … dress is all part of the play?" he asked, waving a hand toward her.

She glanced down at her dress and nodded her head. How could she have forgotten they were all still in costume? She thought about explaining again how the murder mystery weekend worked and why the guests looked like extras in historical movies—though not the same one—but she decided against it. He was a detective; it was his job to deduce.

"It was more of a costume party," she said. There. That was a good answer.

Detective Frost cocked his head. "Why were the lights cut?"

"Well, in reality, I'm not sure what made them go out so early. It's a mystery." Julie did her best to ignore the detective's stern frown. "But in theory, Hannah was supposed to turn out the dining room lights for a few seconds. When they came back on, Inga was going to pretend she was dead. But the lights went out too soon. When we realized Hannah hadn't turned the lights off, Daniel and I went to find the breaker box."

"Daniel Franklin." His frown deepened as he said the name. "How long do you suppose the lights were out?"

Julie thought about it for a moment. "Twenty minutes maybe. Long enough for us to get our bearings, find a flashlight, go upstairs, check that box, and then return to the main box down here."

"Here?"

She pointed to the corner of the tearoom where the main breaker box was located.

The detective turned to one of the uniformed officers hovering by the door. Julie wasn't positive, but it seemed that every peace officer in the area had shown up for this one. "We need to dust that breaker box for prints."

Great. "Daniel and I both touched that," she said.

Detective Frost nodded.

"Has the coroner been called?" she asked.

"Yes." The detective smiled grimly at her. "I know how to do my job, Miss Ellis."

Best not to respond to that. "How long is she, Alice, going to be … uh … here?"

Frost looked at his watch. "Hard to say. Couple of hours. Maybe more."

A couple of hours?

"It's going to take a while for us to get all the prints and process the crime scene," the detective continued. "Then we'll remove the body and notify the next of kin."

Julie shivered. "She's got a couple of kids. Adult kids."

"Husband?"

She shook her head. "Divorced."

"Well, he'll have to be notified too," Frost said.

"What about my guests?"

"Everyone will need to come down to the station to be fingerprinted."

"What's this? We're going to be *fingerprinted*?" Sadie called from her nearby chair.

"Well, I never!" Joyce exclaimed. "Treating us like a bunch of common criminals."

A chorus of grumbles joined in from around the room.

Frost did not appear pleased. "Folks, this is standard procedure and completely necessary. It's as much to eliminate you as suspects as anything else. We will transport you to the police station and bring you all back to the inn when we're done."

"Then what?" Gregory asked. Of all the guests, he appeared to be the angriest. Julie couldn't tell if it was because an inconvenient murder had ruined his weekend plans or if he just had something against cops.

"Then we investigate," said the detective. "No one leaves town for the next seventy-two hours."

"You have got to be kidding me!" Gregory's face turned redder with each word he spoke. "You can't keep us all here for seventy-two hours."

The detective cocked a brow in the man's direction. "Actually, I can."

"But that's not right," Gregory protested. "Making us stay here with a murderer on the loose. There's no telling which one of us might be next."

Susan let out a gasp at his cryptic words. The poor woman was clearly distraught.

Julie wished there was something she could do to make her feel less anxious—to make everyone feel less anxious. Except for the killer, of course. That monster didn't deserve to be treated so kindly. If only she knew who the monster was.

"I need to lie down," Susan choked.

Kenneth patted her on the back reassuringly. He whispered something in her ear, and she nodded. Whatever he said appeared to calm her, if only a bit.

Joyce and Sadie also seemed to calm down.

"Will we still be able to quilt, dear?" Sadie asked.

"I don't see why not." Julie looked to the detective

He remained expressionless and then shrugged.

"Well, I say, this sure puts a new spin on things." Kenneth seemed more than a little excited by the gruesome turn of events. Given his previous *dis*interest in everything, Julie found his heightened enthusiasm odd at best.

The only remaining guests who hadn't sounded off at the detective were Liam and Carrie. Julie looked to the young blonde. "Do you have any questions?" she asked.

"If we have to stay, we have to stay," Carrie said.

Despite her shaky voice, Julie thought she caught a look of relief in the girl's eyes. But there was no time to dwell on it. "Dr. Preston?"

Liam Preston continued to stare at the table in front of him. Julie could almost hear the wheels turning in his head.

"Dr. Preston?" she repeated.

"What?" Liam seemed to snap out of his stupor. "Oh, yes, if the law requires it ..."

"I still say this bites." Gregory crossed his arms over his ample chest and glared at the detective.

It seemed Frost was accustomed to such looks. He simply turned away and addressed the group as a whole. "I expect everyone to remain here until Monday night. You are free to move about the town, but you're not free to leave. Anyone caught trying to skip town before I release you will be arrested for obstructing justice. Are we understood?"

A murmur of reluctant agreement went up all around.

"Does that mean we're arrested?" Kenneth asked. He actually seemed excited by the idea.

"I've never been arrested before," Sadie said in amazement.

"Me neither," Joyce chimed in.

"No one is arrested," Frost explained. "But you are all on the short list of suspects."

"But isn't it possible that someone else entered the building at some point and committed the crime?" Liam asked.

"Absolutely," Frost said. "We'll be looking at all possibilities."

Julie was not looking forward to calling the inn's owner and trying to explain to her that another murder had happened in their sleepy little town, and this one in her very own inn! Millie would be beside herself. Julie decided then and there to handle it herself. That was why she was in charge. Millie could find out when she returned home. Plus, there wasn't anything she could do from Baja anyway.

"What do we do now?" Susan asked. The poor woman looked like she needed a tranquilizer and a two-day nap.

"Remain right where you are until I come back," Frost said. "I need to talk with Miss Ellis in private. Then we'll all drive down to the station together. Any questions?"

The guests shook their heads.

Detective Frost led Julie to the front sitting area. He sat awkwardly on the small sofa and motioned for her to join him.

Julie perched on the edge of the couch, unwilling to get too comfortable or to let her guard down where Everett Frost was concerned.

"Tell me what you know about each of your guests," he started without preamble.

"Not a lot. We don't require them to fill out background checks before they stay here." Though Julie thought it might not be a bad idea going forward.

"Surely you learned something about them in the time that they've been here."

"Well, Sadie and Joyce are best friends. Sadie is a retired librarian, and Joyce is a widowed housewife. They've been saving for this trip for years."

"Did either one of them act as if they knew our victim?"

Julie thought for a moment. "No."

"What about the married couple?"

"I think I overheard him say that he's a podiatrist."

Frost nodded grimly. "No wonder this seemed like a good time to him."

"You noticed that too?"

"It's my job to pay attention to details, Miss Ellis."

"Right. Well, they have grown children in college. This is the first vacation they've taken in years. To be honest, when they first arrived, Kenneth seemed like he'd rather poke himself in the eye with a fork than be here."

"What about the professor, Liam Preston?"

"Dr. Preston didn't say very much during tea."

"I see. And where does he teach?"

"One of the state universities ... I think. I can look at his registration if you'd like."

Frost waved away her offer and continued. "What about Gregory?"

"All I remember him saying was that one day he was going to move down to Belize and live like a king."

"Did any of the other guests seem to know the victim?"

Julie thought back. "Alice sat at the table with Carrie Windsor—"

"The little one?"

"Yes. But they didn't talk much. Carrie's quiet and Alice ...," she faltered, "Alice seemed bitter."

"Did you overhear anyone say anything about her?"

"Not much. Just that her kids bought her this weekend to cheer her up after her divorce."

"Was it a bad marriage?"

"I don't know." Julie frowned. "Good ones don't end in divorce though, do they?"

Frost quirked a brow.

"Alice acted like she didn't want to be here. I thought that was strange. A weekend here isn't exactly cheap, and then with the murder mystery on top of that ..."

"Did she have a job that you know of?"

"I'm not sure."

"And Carrie," Frost said, "what about her?"

"She arrived last. That's all I know. She's very quiet. I think she's a student."

"She told you this?" he asked.

"No."

"You heard her tell someone else?"

"No, but—"

"So, you don't really know if she's a student or not?"

Julie shook her head, wondering when this had turned into an interrogation. "Should I call my attorney?" She should have said *an* attorney. It wasn't like she had a lawyer on retainer ready to bail her out of such situations.

"It might not be a bad idea, given the complicated situation, murder on your premises and all that. I'm sure Millie has someone she uses for other things."

"Is that all?" Julie asked hopefully.

Detective Frost flipped his little notebook closed. "For now," he said. "You will all be transported to the station for prints and brought back in as timely a manner as possible. We'll finish up here as quickly as we can, but no one will be allowed in the dining room until we're done in there."

Great. Power failure, murder, and no one could eat in the dining room. It was going to be a red-letter weekend for sure.

As promised, the guests were taken by van to the police station and fingerprinted individually. Then they all returned to the van and were driven back to the inn.

They received several strange looks while at the station. It was one thing to be dressed in costumes in the privacy of the inn, but to have to go out into public—even worse, to the police station—well, that was more than any of them were prepared for.

The atmosphere on both trips was strained. Julie could almost feel the accusations running through everyone's minds.

Only Kenneth seemed blissfully immune to the tense atmosphere around them. "Don't get me wrong," he told Julie after they were back at the inn, "but this is far more interesting than a murder play."

Julie wondered if he really felt that way or if he was trying to bait the others with his weird comments.

"Someone died," Susan scolded. "This isn't cause for celebration."

"You're right about that," Liam agreed. "But it is also rather interesting. Like *CSI*, but for real."

"I, for one, think it's terrible," Joyce said with a sniff. "And I'm more than a little nervous being cooped up with the likes of all of you. *Someone* killed the woman."

"I still say it's possible that the killer sneaked in, did the deed, and then sneaked back out," Kenneth said.

"It's all so very sad," Sadie said, shaking her head.

"It isn't like we knew her or anything," Kenneth said.

Susan swatted his am. "It doesn't matter if we knew her or not, she was still a person. It's a terrible thing."

"What's terrible is them keeping us here like a bunch of caged animals," Gregory said.

"Oh please. Did any of you even know the woman's last name?" Kenneth asked, looking around at each of them, almost daring someone to answer.

"Peyton," Julie supplied in a cold voice. "Her last name was Peyton." Kenneth's enthusiasm rubbed her the wrong way. She could only hope this was how he relieved stress.

"Who cares what her last name was?" Gregory asked. "We shouldn't be made to stay here while the Keystone Cops run around and try to blame all of us for her death."

Susan's eyes widened. She turned to her husband and whispered something in his ear.

Kenneth merely shrugged.

Susan sat back in her seat, looking a bit stunned.

"I mean, let's be honest. One of us probably killed the woman," Gregory said. "No one snuck in and back out undetected. That's just wishful thinking. And now we have to stay locked up together for seventy-two hours, knowing that one of us is a murderer. I don't know about you, but I'm ready to call my attorney." Gregory scanned all their faces as if looking for an ally in the group.

"Should we?" Joyce asked, looking at Julie.

"But I don't have an attorney," Sadie murmured. "I've never needed one." Her hands fidgeted in her lap, making Julie wonder if she quilted when she was upset. If that was the case, the quilt project would be finished with time to spare.

"Let's not be hasty," Daniel broke in. "All of this speculation and talk of attorneys isn't solving anything. Let's wait to see what the police find." His deep voice was reassuring to Julie, whose nerves had grown more frayed with each passing minute.

"I agree," Liam said. "Until we know more, we should assume that everyone here is innocent and let the police handle it. For all we know, her ex-husband broke into the inn and killed her so he didn't have to pay alimony. Or maybe she managed to fall and hit her own head on that candlestick."

Gregory scoffed. "Sure, you go ahead and believe that fairy tale if it makes you feel better."

Anxious murmurs rippled through the room.

Julie noticed that Carrie remained quiet through the entire conversation. The young girl kept her bespectacled eyes down and studied her chewed-up nails as if her life depended on it.

As Julie glanced around at the other faces, from the worried frowns of Sadie and Joyce to the shocked smile plastered across Susan's anxious features, an unsettling thought occurred to her: If one of the guests *hadn't* killed Alice Peyton, then one of her staff most likely had.

FOUR

Julie stood and clinked her spoon against her juice glass. "If I could have everyone's attention please." Breakfast was a tense affair. Most of the guests had been in various states of shock since the prior evening, but in the light of the morning, fresh suspicions and conspiracy theories reared their ugly heads.

"I know the events of last night still have everyone a bit shaken," Julie said. She was thinking about Shirley, who was still so unnerved. "But since everyone is here and has to remain in town," Julie continued, "I see no reason not to move ahead with our original quilting plan. It might help to ease some stress."

"About that," Gregory started. "I don't see why I should have to pay for my room since I'm required to stay here now, and your security seems less than adequate."

There's always one.

"Mr. Wilson," Julie began, "I do apologize for the inconvenience, but given our present circumstances and the fact that we are a business, I feel it's more appropriate to focus on the positives and continue with our weekend plans as best we can. You most certainly will not be charged for the murder mystery portion of the weekend."

He snorted. "So, no full refunds is what you're saying."

Julie took a deep breath to keep from losing her cool.

"We're still going to quilt," Sadie said, which brought a stern look from Gregory. "I do find it relaxing."

"I think that sounds like a lovely idea," Joyce agreed.

Susan sniffed as if she might start crying again at any moment.

"I agree it might be a good stress reliever. Despite everything," Julie said, "I'd still like to present one of you with the quilt come Monday when you're able to leave town. Are we all in agreement?"

Most of the guests agreed.

"And no more murders, right?" Susan asked. "Not even pretend ones?"

"No more murders." Julie uttered the words she hoped would prove true.

Shortly after breakfast, everyone headed out for historic home tours, wine tasting at the vineyards, and walking tours of the quaint town. The guests seemed more than anxious to get away from the inn for a while, and Julie couldn't blame them.

Since she didn't have to man the front desk, she shut herself in her office and called Detective Frost. He was definitely a bulldog, but this time his tenacity might benefit her if he could shed some light on the events of the previous evening.

"Julie Ellis, what a surprise," he drawled. He didn't sound at all surprised. More like he had been waiting all morning for her call.

"I have a couple of questions about last night." She drummed her fingers against her desk and waited impatiently for his answer.

"You know I can't discuss an open case with you."

"Of course not," Julie said as sweetly as possible, "and I wouldn't ask you to. It's just," she exhaled audibly, hoping to elicit sympathy from Frost, "I have seven people here who are very worried about the situation. Can you tell me anything that would help me reassure them?"

He let out a long sigh. "I'll tell you what I can. But if I can't answer, I can't answer."

"Fair enough," she said. "Has the coroner determined the cause of death?"

"You need the coroner's report to tell you that?"

Julie supposed she deserved that. Alice had been found facedown next to a heavy blunt object, with a knot the size of St. Louis on the back of her head. "The candlestick," she muttered.

"Does it belong to the inn?"

"Yes. Well, we've owned it for a week. It was a prop for the murder mystery."

There was silence on the other end of the line.

"You know, 'with the candlestick in the dining room,' like in the board game Clue," Julie added.

"Are you saying it was your fake murder weapon?"

"Yes and no." She closed her eyes, fighting the headache that was starting to form.

"Why don't you tell me more about this weekend you had planned."

Julie sighed. How many times would he ask her the same question? Was he trying to trip her up or catch her in some lie? Why she'd thought he would be any help to her was the real mystery. "It was simple, really. All the guests were supposed to determine who killed Inga."

"And she was supposed to be hit on the head with a giant candlestick?" Frost asked.

"No, she was supposed to drink poisoned wine."

"The wine was poisoned too?"

"Not really poisoned," she said. "The wine was fine. We added almond extract to it to make it smell like it had been tainted with arsenic. Inga was supposed to drink it even though it was meant for Shirley. No one was supposed to get hit in the head." *Especially not Alice.*

"If Inga was your victim, who was supposed to have killed her?"

"Daniel."

"Ah, Franklin. I should have known he'd have some part in this."

"Daniel didn't *do* anything," Julie said.

"Are you sure about that?"

Julie bristled at the detective's accusatory tone. "Positive. He was with me the entire time." She'd told Frost all of this the night before, and she'd had enough of the conversation. She felt like a dog chasing its tail. "You know what? I've got to get back to work."

"Of course."

She sighed. "Why do you hate me?" She nearly slapped a hand over her mouth. She hadn't meant to say that out loud.

Across the line, she could almost hear his grimacing smile. "And there's where you're wrong, Miss Ellis. I don't hate you at all."

"We're looking for Julie Ellis." The young man read her name off the card he held in one hand. He stood just inside the door of the inn, looking sorely out of place in a pair of denim overalls and a sport coat. Two women flanked him, one on each side. They were dressed a little nicer, but something about them both screamed "country." One wore slacks and a button-down shirt, the other a flower-print dress reminiscent of Alice Kramden, from the old TV show *The Honeymooners*, might wear.

"I'm Julie," she said, walking around the registration desk. "How can I help you?"

The man's blue eyes filled with tears, but he sniffed them back. There was something familiar about the way he held his chin and the downward turn to the corners of his mouth. "I'm Rusty Peyton. Alice is—was my mother." He mopped his face with a handkerchief. The woman to his left stifled a sob, while the one on his right remained stoic and cool.

"Mr. Peyton," Julie said, taking his handkerchief-free hand into her own. She felt the card he read from earlier crease beneath her grasp. "I am so sorry for your loss."

He dropped his head and wiped at his face again. "Thank you. The police said we could come by here and pick up her things. We're taking her home this afternoon."

The dark-haired woman on his left, the one wearing the dress, sobbed again, a choked and strangled sound.

"This is my wife, Serena Peyton," he said, indicating the bereft woman. "And this is my sister, Amelia Peyton."

Bleach-blond Amelia shot Julie a twist of her mouth that Julie could only assume was meant to be a smile of greeting. It was more on the side of a grimace.

"Can we get on with this?" Amelia asked, eyeing her surroundings as if she had somehow found herself at the city dump. "This place gives me the creeps."

Julie blinked. Not exactly the response one would expect from a girl who had just lost her mother. "Of course."

Amelia turned to glare at Julie. "Your inn is clearly not a safe place to be. *You* failed to protect my mother."

Julie blinked again and then turned to the less hostile Rusty Peyton. "Nothing like this has ever happened here before."

"Like that helps anyone now," Amelia said over Serena's continued sobs. "Our mother is dead!"

"I'm so sorry for your loss," Julie said again. It was all she could say, though she knew it was weak. What was the protocol for an inn manager who was faced with the family of a murdered guest? Someone should write an etiquette book on it—*Avoiding Awkward Innkeeper Interactions.* Maybe she would. "Let me get the key, and I'll show you to her room."

A horrified look crossed Rusty's face, and he shook his head. Like Alice, he had brown hair, though his wasn't streaked with gray. "No ma'am," he said. "I don't think I can pick up her things like that."

"Oh, for pity's sake, I'll do it," Amelia said, snatching the key out of Julie's hand as she stood there, stunned. She knew grief could get angry, but it was still shocking to see.

In one quick swipe, Rusty took the key from his sister and deposited it back in Julie's hand. "Miss Ellis, would you do us the favor of gathering our mother's things?"

It was unorthodox, to be sure, but gathering Alice Peyton's things might offer a clue or two about who killed her. The police had already searched her room the night of the murder, of course, gathering any clues that they could. But maybe they had missed one.

Julie closed her fingers around the key and smiled reassuringly at Rusty. "Of course I will. In the meantime, why don't you make yourselves comfortable in the tearoom?" She ushered them into Shirley's place, which was nearly full.

"Shirley, please give Alice Peyton's family anything they want, on me."

"You got it." Shirley was busy working behind the counter but paused to give the family a sympathetic look, which was met by a judgmental stare from Amelia. Julie guessed it was inspired by Shirley's outfit, which made her look like a wayward gypsy—handmade handkerchief skirt, matching hat, and patchwork vest in bright shades of purple and red.

As the Peytons settled in at the last available table, Julie joined Shirley at the counter to find out why the tearoom was so crowded.

"It's been like this since the mur—since I opened." Shirley caught herself before she actually said the word. And for that, Julie was grateful. She didn't think the sobbing Serena Peyton could stand to hear it.

"I'll be back down in a few minutes," Julie said. "I can give you a hand if you need it."

Shirley smiled gratefully. "I'll holler at Hannah if I get in over my head."

Julie nodded and turned back to the Peyton trio. "I'll be back as soon as I can."

The bell over the door tinkled as Julie passed by on her way to Alice's room, warning that another visitor had entered the inn. She smiled absently in the man's direction and then did a double take. Tall and blond, there was something familiar about him. It was a subtle déjà vu, as if she'd seen him before but never actually met him.

He smiled in return, but his eyes remained sad.

"May I help you?" she asked.

"No, thank you. Just meeting someone." He headed in the direction of the tearoom.

Julie cast him one last look before heading up to the second floor. Her stilettos clicked against the stairs as she climbed. Out of habit, she knocked on the door before shaking her head and letting herself in.

She fully expected to walk into a room that looked like it had been rifled through by the police—drawers hanging open, possessions strewn about. But the room was immaculate. Everything looked neat as could be. All the drawers were in place, the closet door shut. The bed had been stripped and clean sheets were placed at the foot of the mattress, waiting for the next guest to arrive.

Inga, housekeeper extraordinaire, strikes again.

Julie spotted Alice's suitcase and overnight bag sitting off to one side. Inga had even packed the woman's bags, knowing eventually the family would come for them.

Of course, the family didn't know they were already packed.

Julie quickly lifted the overnight case onto the bed and unzipped the top. Shampoo, deodorant, and toothpaste—nothing special there. Even Alice's makeup bag was filled with ordinary, everyday cosmetics. Then again, what was Julie expecting to find? A note that said, "In case I'm murdered, know that so-and-so is responsible"?

She sighed and closed the overnight bag. Then she lifted the suitcase to the bed and unhooked the latches. It was a hard-sided style from the eighties with fake satin interior and an elastic pocket sewn into the top.

All of Alice's clothes were stacked inside so neatly that Julie was almost loath to disturb them. Almost. She reached inside and ran her fingers over the material. Jeans, a sweater, slacks, shirts, one dress, and three pairs of shoes.

How was she planning to survive the weekend with only three pairs of shoes?

Other than the lack of footwear, she found nothing remarkable in the case. Julie ran her hands inside the elastic pouch and brought out a newspaper from the city of Little Rock, the *Arkansas News Today*. It wasn't the entire paper. At least Julie didn't think so. It was about the same thickness as the Straussberg paper, and her little Missouri town was much smaller than Little Rock, Arkansas. The portion of paper was folded in half and included the front page. There was an article about a kids' museum opening and the new tax initiative that had been passed. Nothing incredibly noteworthy. At least not from where Julie was standing. She unfolded it and glanced at the back. One headline in particular jumped out at her: "Rare Find in Missouri B&B."

It appeared to be the same article written about the Quilt Haus Inn that had run a few days earlier in the local Straussberg paper. This meant Alice had known about the journal before she came to Missouri.

Yet, she'd seemed so disinterested when I brought out the journal for everyone to see.

Julie thought for a moment. Maybe it was all a coincidence. After all, what would a nearly worthless Civil War journal have to do with Alice's murder? It was possible that Alice hadn't even noticed the article hidden on the back page.

Julie tucked the newspaper back into its pocket and neatly repacked Alice's suitcase. She latched the case, gathered both bags, and headed out of the room. She'd ponder the newspaper article discovery later. Right now, she had a grieving family to deal with.

She carted the cases down the stairs and left them by the front desk.

She heard Shirley telling a story to a group of guests as she walked into the tearoom. The amount of gossip that found its way into the woman's "historical" talks was nothing short of a miracle.

"I have your mother's things at the front desk when you're ready," Julie said to the Peytons. "But there's no rush. Take all the time you need."

Rusty stood, stretched his long legs, and gave her a grateful, watery smile. "Thank you, ma'am. We appreciate that, but it's time for us to get her back home."

Julie followed them to the front of the inn.

"Is this everything?" Rusty asked, gesturing toward the bags on the floor.

Julie nodded. He picked up both bags; then, realizing that he didn't have his hand free to shake hers, sat the large suitcase on the ground and clasped her hand in his large callused one. "Thank you for your help, Miss Ellis."

"You're most welcome." But somehow that didn't seem to be quite enough. She needed to say something reassuring. "I'm sure your mother really appreciated you arranging this trip for her."

Serena sobbed, Amelia rolled her eyes, and Rusty looked confused.

"We didn't buy her this trip," he said. Then his voice turned sour. "Her boyfriend did."

Julie frowned. "I thought she said that she was recently divorced, and her children paid for this trip as a present to her."

"Well, ma'am," Rusty said, "I don't know why she would say something like that. Or maybe you just misunderstood. Our father died when we were in elementary school. Mother never remarried. There was no divorce."

After the Peytons left, Julie went about her daily inn duties, still thinking about the bizarre circumstances surrounding Alice Peyton. She checked the account ledgers, paid a couple of bills, and unclogged a toilet on the second floor.

Ah, the glamorous life of an innkeeper, she thought as she booted up her computer.

"Julie!" Inga's staunch accent stiffened Julie's spine. Something in the woman's tone told Julie that whatever she had to say was not going to be good. "Something must be done."

Julie pasted on a look of concern as Inga stormed toward the front desk. She closed her laptop and gave the housekeeper her full attention. "What's wrong?"

The housekeeper's cheeks were stained with pink, and the normally starched perfection that defined Inga seemed less pronounced than usual. Her hands fluttered about in uncharacteristic agitation. "These gawkers! They come in, leave their trash, put fingerprints on everything, and then they leave. They're running me in circles."

"Julie?" Shirley called out, marching toward the desk, an annoyed expression on her face. "You have *got* to do something."

"So I've been told." Julie rubbed at her temples. "What's wrong?" Her look of concern was already turning into one of irritation.

"All of these people! They're coming in and hovering around, but they're not buying anything." Shirley shook her head. "I'm not talking one or two. There are dozens of them. You saw how packed it was this morning."

"Not just this morning. All day it's been like this." Inga grimaced. "They want to see the police tape and the candlestick."

"I hope you told them the candlestick is in the police evidence room," Julie said.

Inga crossed her arms and tapped her foot. "I tell them *nothing*."

The bell above the door chimed as someone else entered the inn. It had been going off nonstop all day. But Straussberg was a tourist town; without the tourists there was no trade.

"I know we need customers in the shop, but I don't like the kind of people that have been coming in today," Shirley said. "Something needs to be done. I can hardly take care of my real customers, thanks to all the others milling around just so they can claim they've been to a real murder scene." She paused. "I suppose if they at least bought *something* that would be better."

"And make it even harder on the kitchen," Inga replied sharply.

Julie waved a hand to indicate the conversation was at its close. "I'm sorry, ladies. I know how difficult this is, but let's be patient. We can't afford to offend locals or tourists who might recommend the inn to a potential customer."

"For all the wrong reasons," Shirley said under her breath.

"This will die down soon. I'm betting by tomorrow."

Inga grunted her dissatisfaction. "At least put a sign on the door that says gawkers aren't welcome. Or maybe a two-cookie maximum for the tearoom."

"I think you mean a two-cookie minimum," Shirley said.

Inga just glared at her.

"I'll give it some thought," Julie said.

Inga harrumphed again and left the room.

"Do you really think this will die down soon?" Shirley asked as a family of four brushed past, the woman snapping pictures as she herded her children in front of her.

Julie managed a smile. "I know so. Until then, just keep being your charming self. Things will smooth out in no time."

I hope.

Shirley gave a quick nod. "You're the boss."

Rusty Peyton's comment had truly thrown Julie for a loop. The man had just lost his last remaining parent, and Julie wasn't about to dispute his words about who'd paid for his mother's trip. But why would Alice lie about herself—and did it have anything to do with her untimely demise?

It occurred to Julie that if she wanted information about her guests, she was going to have to get it on her own. Detective Frost certainly wasn't going to be any help, if her conversation with him earlier in the day was any indication.

The guests were all out enjoying the town, so Julie chose the next best thing to direct questioning. She booted up her computer and punched in the first guest's name.

"Knock, knock." Hannah was standing in the doorway with a plate of pastries.

"Come in, especially if those treats are for me." Julie leaned back in her chair and eyed the plate. "Is that what I think it is?"

"I thought you could use a little culinary pick-me-up." Hannah shrugged, but Julie had a feeling her friend was near to bursting with pride. "Millie thought it would be good to play up the whole German town thing."

Julie forked off a piece of the flaky cinnamon strudel and didn't even try to stifle her moan of pleasure as she took a bite.

Hannah looked uncharacteristically pleased with herself.

"This is almost as good as pickles and caramel," Julie teased, knowing Hannah was repulsed by Julie's comfort food of choice.

Hannah scrunched her nose. "This is so much better."

"You're right." Julie said. "And if you keep this up, I'll gain twenty pounds by fall." She took another bite and sighed as the pastry melted in her mouth.

Hannah settled into a nearby chair and watched Julie eat.

"You really missed your calling, you know that?" Julie said.

"How so?"

"You should have been cooking professionally long ago."

Hannah tucked her feet underneath her. "Maybe. I am

really enjoying it." She waited a heartbeat before continuing. "Is this going to mess everything up?"

"This?"

"The murder."

"Absolutely not." Julie shook her head, though she wasn't as certain as she pretended to be. Still she knew how badly her friend wanted to remain in Straussberg. Hannah had fully embraced life in small-town Missouri. "Everything is going to be fine."

Hannah grimaced. "You know what I mean. Do you think this was the work of the ...? Well, you know. Do you think they mistook Alice for you?"

Julie was a good three inches taller than Alice Peyton, and she hadn't been in the room for most of the time the power was out. But she *had* been there when Alice was struck.

"I don't think I was the target, if that's what you mean." Even as Julie said the words, worry seeped into her thoughts. It had been dark in the dining room. Very dark.

"Have you been investigating?" Hannah nodded toward the computer.

"Just got started."

"Anything interesting come up?"

"Not yet." Julie took another bite of the pastry and then set the plate on her desk. A couple of clicks later the face of her first guest filled the screen. "Gregory Wilson was arrested," Julie said with some alarm. "He took a rare baseball card from a store in Montana."

"Did he go to jail for it?"

"Yeah, looks like he did. He was also accused of stealing a painting in California, but those charges were dropped."

"Well, theft and murder are worlds apart," Hannah pointed out.

Julie just raised an eyebrow at Hannah and typed in another name. "Sadie Davidson is a retired librarian. She never married and has three cats. She and Joyce have been friends since grade school. Joyce was recently widowed when her husband died of a heart attack."

"We knew all this already."

Julie nodded. "Both are on a fixed income."

"And that is suspect how?" Hannah asked.

"Well, it's a little strange. There are cheaper places to stay in the area than the Quilt Haus Inn. It didn't have to be their first choice for a simple vacation."

"But think about it," Hannah said. "All Sadie has talked about since she got here is quilting. And they get two meals a day included in the weekend's special price as well as the evening entertainment. Even with a more expensive room rate, it's a pretty good deal."

"I suppose. They *did* mention that a murder mystery was on their bucket list," Julie conceded. Before she dismissed them from suspicion, she scanned the screen for any information she might have missed. "What about this? Joyce lost all of her money in a Ponzi scheme."

"All of it?" Hannah's eyes were wide with surprise.

"She's a complainant in a lawsuit against an investment company, but there aren't too many details about it."

"If she lost all of her money, then how did she pay for this?"

Julie shrugged. "Sadie?"

"Maybe. What about … Alice Peyton?" Hannah hesitated briefly before saying the woman's name.

Julie couldn't say she blamed her friend. They'd both seen a lot in their years recovering stolen antiquities, but never anything so morbid this close to home. She typed "Alice Peyton" into the search engine, and several hits came up. Julie chose the one that looked like the Alice that had been staying with them at the inn. "Single, mother of two, worked for a man named Eric Rutherford from Rutherford International."

"What of kind company is that?"

Julie shrugged. "It doesn't say." So why did it sound so familiar? She leaned back in her seat and forked up another bite of the strudel.

"Why are you frowning at my strudel?" Hannah demanded.

"That name. It sounds so familiar." Julie tapped her fork on the plate as she tried to remember. Then it hit her. "Eric Rutherford is the expert I called to appraise the Civil War journal."

"Are you sure?"

"Positive." Julie typed his name into the search engine. "Yep. Same one." Which meant Alice definitely knew about the journal when she came to the inn. The newspaper section in her suitcase was no fluke. But what would any of that have to do with murder?

"I guess this is too bizarre to be a coincidence," Hannah said, her brows furrowed.

"And the story gets weirder."

"How so?"

"Alice's family came by this morning. They were a strange bunch, to say the least." Julie recounted the odd trio who had shown up to get Alice's bags. "And then they told me that they didn't buy her this weekend trip. They claimed her boyfriend bought it for her—and she wasn't divorced, but widowed."

"Why would Alice lie about something like that?" Hannah asked.

"That's what I've been trying to figure out. It's a weird lie to tell. Her son said maybe I misunderstood, but I vividly remember her saying that."

Hannah nodded and then waited as Julie tapped away at the keyboard.

"Kenneth and Susan Calhoun," Julie announced the names of the next two guests. "He's an overworked podiatrist. She's a housewife and part-time office manager for Kenneth's practice. Mother of three."

"Exactly who they claimed to be?" Hannah asked.

"Almost too much so," Julie muttered.

"Don't let your imagination get the better of you," Hannah warned. "Stick to the facts."

"Well, we have to conjecture a little," Julie said. "And there's something not right about those two."

"Yeah, they're terrible," Hannah said, rolling her eyes dramatically. "People who have nothing to hide are the *worst*."

Julie shot her an annoyed look and continued. "They have three children—two boys and a girl. All three are in college."

"And?"

"His website says he extended his hours of operation as of last year. Maybe the doctor is trying to make ends meet. He did say this is the first vacation he's had in three years." Which proved absolutely nothing.

"So, that's it on them?" Hannah asked.

"No," Julie said, holding up a finger. "Susan's father was an art collector. Nothing big though." It was the closest thing to a connection she had. She wondered if Susan Calhoun's tie to the art world could be relevant.

"And Carrie?" Hannah asked.

"I can't find Carrie at all."

"Really?"

Julie shrugged. "Nineteen listings pop up, but only three are in Missouri. And none matched the picture of our Carrie Windsor."

"Where did she say she was from?" Hannah asked.

"Kansas City." Julie drummed her fingers on the desk. "But maybe she meant Kansas City, *Kansas*." Julie searched, but there were no listings in Kansas. "Huh."

"Perhaps 'Carrie' is short for something. Like 'Carolina.'"

"Could be," Julie said. "But it could just as easily be short for something else."

"That only leaves the handsome Dr. Liam Preston."

"Right." Julie typed his name into the search engine window and scanned the results list that appeared on her screen. "Do you suppose Liam is short for William?"

Hannah raised her brows. "No idea. Why?"

"Liam Preston lives in New York with his two Yorkies and his very young assistant. He's eighty-four years old."

"That doesn't sound like the Liam Preston staying here. He said he was a professor at a university in Missouri, right?"

Julie was just about to close out the browser window when a name caught her attention. She clicked on the link and then read the screen twice to make sure she truly understood. "Well, that explains why he could never remember to answer when someone called his name."

"What do you mean?"

"Liam Preston is none other than L.P. Wallis," Julie said.

Hannah stared at her blankly. "And this is supposed to mean something to me?"

"L.P. Wallis? One of the hottest mystery writers around."

The statement had no more than passed through Julie's lips when a scream rang out.

FIVE

In an instant, Julie and Hannah were both on their feet. They raced out of the office as the scream sounded again.

"It sounded like it came from upstairs," Hannah said.

Despite her very high heels, Julie took the stairs two at a time, leaving the shorter Hannah to scramble behind.

"It's in there!" Susan screeched at Julie. She stood outside the shared bathroom on the second floor with one hand clamped over her mouth, her eyes wide and fearful. She pointed toward the open door. "Get it!"

Kenneth hovered in the doorway of their room, rubbing his eyes as if he'd just awoken.

"Get what?" Julie asked, inching toward the bathroom door. She wasn't too keen on going inside until she knew what she was up against.

"The snake!"

Julie shot Hannah a look.

Hannah quickly wrapped one arm around Susan's waist and led her away from the bathroom door before she could scream again.

Joyce poked her head out of the room she shared with Sadie and asked, "What happened?"

Julie managed a smile. "Nothing. Just a small issue in the bathroom." That had to be the lamest excuse she'd ever offered.

"Oh," Joyce said, looking more than a little relieved. "My Alvin used to be a plumber. You want me to take a look?"

"Thank you for offering, but I think I'll let the experts handle this."

"Handle what?" Sadie pushed past her friend and joined the growing fray in the hallway.

"Just a little issue." Julie cautiously peered inside the bathroom. *Please let it be a rubber snake. Please let it be a rubber snake. Please let it be a rubber snake.*

No such luck. Coiled up inside the bathtub was a thick black snake, its eyes an evil yellow. They seemed to glow in the flat, dark face that stared up at Julie, its tongue flickering and tasting the air around it.

Her heart flip-flopped in her chest. She wasn't *scared* of snakes, but she surely didn't want to mess with them if she didn't have to.

"Is there really a snake in there?" Kenneth had finally managed to wake up enough to comprehend what was happening. He stood behind Julie and peered over her shoulder.

"There is indeed a snake," she grimly replied.

"A snake?" Joyce repeated, creeping up behind them. "A venomous one?"

Julie shrugged. She didn't know a great deal about snakes, and she didn't really want to find out.

"Kenneth," she said, unwilling to take her eyes off the snake for more than a couple of seconds, "will you please go downstairs and get the phone off the reception desk? I think we need to call a critter guy."

Kenneth scratched his head. "Critter guy?" He still sounded a little groggy.

"Wildlife removal service," she explained.

"Oh." He looked over his shoulder toward his suite.

"If you'd rather see to your wife, that's fine. Just send Hannah."

Kenneth nodded and left the room as Julie continued to face down the snake. Thankfully, the serpent didn't appear too active or ready to strike. Julie supposed that it was probably cool and comfortable on the porcelain.

Hannah appeared in the hallway and caught Julie's eye. "I'm on it," she said before disappearing down the stairs.

Neither Julie nor the snake moved as they waited for the critter guy to arrive. After what seemed like an eternity—but was probably less than ten minutes—Julie heard pounding footsteps on the stairs.

"What's going on?" Gregory demanded.

Just the person she didn't need.

"There's a snake in the bathtub," Liam said.

Julie wondered when *he'd* joined the party.

"We don't know what kind," Joyce chimed in. "It could be deadly."

"I don't suspect it is," Julie said.

"A *snake*?" Gregory blustered. "Now see here, the situation in this ... this hotel of horrors has gotten way out of hand! What if one of us had been bitten? Can you imagine? Another dead body at the inn! Something has to be done."

"Something is being done." Julie struggled to keep her voice civil. "A wildlife removal specialist is on his way here to get rid of the snake."

Julie had braced herself for more complaints when heavy footsteps on the staircase preempted Gregory's newest attempt to get out of paying his bill.

"You have a snake up here?" an unfamiliar male voice asked.

Thank heavens! "In here!"

A large, burly man stuck his head in the bathroom.

"Thank you for coming so fast," Julie said, moving away from the tub to give him room.

The man pointed over his shoulder. "I was down at the end of the block, so I came right over."

"Is it poisonous?" Sadie asked.

"Nope. Just a black rat snake."

"Is that bad?" Joyce asked. Her voice held a wistful tone.

"It is if you're a rat."

"Oh." Sadie seemed disappointed.

"If it's got round pupils, it's not venomous," the man said. "Just look at those friendly eyes."

"Who's looking at its eyes?" Joyce asked. "I was looking at its flickering tongue."

"I'll get out of your way and leave you to it." Julie stepped out of the room and ushered her guests away from the bathroom door.

Kenneth emerged from his suite and quietly closed the door behind him.

"How's Susan?" Julie asked him.

He placed one finger over his lips. "Resting."

"So, what are we going to do about this incompetent innkeeper?" Gregory's loud voice echoed off the walls in the small space of the hall.

Julie grit her teeth. Either he wasn't trying to be discreet or he didn't have a clue how to be. "We're going to go downstairs to the tearoom," Julie answered, "where we can talk without disturbing Susan." She fixed Gregory with a pointed look, fully expecting him to protest. Instead, he gave her a stiff nod and started down the stairs.

Shirley's eyes widened as everyone made their way into the tearoom. "I thought I heard someone scream," she whispered to Julie. "Did something happen?"

"You could say that."

"So." Gregory crossed his arms over his wide girth and narrowed his eyes at her. "If you and the police are going to force us to stay here, what are you going to do to secure our safety?"

"I am not forcing you to do anything. The police are. And you don't have to stay here. You just have to stay in town."

"But if I leave, you're not giving me a refund, are you?" Gregory challenged.

It was definitely tempting to give in and refund Gregory's money, but she didn't want to give him the satisfaction.

"It says here that black rat snakes will bite if provoked," Joyce interjected. She had her tablet in hand and was furiously surfing the Web.

Well, it's a good thing no one provoked it.

"They aren't venomous," Shirley said. "They're constrictors."

Julie shot her a look.

Shirley just shrugged. "What? I grew up on a farm."

"I think somebody put it in the bathtub to scare us," Joyce said.

"Maybe even bite one of us," Sadie added.

Shirley rolled her eyes.

"Chances are, it crawled in there on its own." The Critter Guy was standing in the doorway with a wriggling bag in his hand. "Rat snakes are climbers. I've taken them out of drain pipes, off of rooftops; even got one out of a chimney once."

Comforting, Julie thought.

"So, if the inn has rat snakes, does that mean it has rats?" Gregory asked.

Julie bit back a retort.

"No," Critter Guy said. "The inn wouldn't have rats with this baby around."

With that, Julie jumped up and escorted Critter Guy to the front door while staying as far from the twitching sack as possible.

"What are the real odds that this fellow crawled in here on his own accord?" Julie asked once they were out of earshot of everyone else.

Critter Guy shot her a reassuring smile. "I'd say it's most likely what happened."

"So, I wouldn't necessarily need to contact the police about it?"

He laughed. "Not unless you want 'em mad at you for wasting their time."

Everyone, minus Susan, was still gathered in the tearoom when Julie went back inside.

"What do we do now?" Liam asked.

A chorus of concerned murmurs followed his question.

Julie held up her hands to stay the protests. "I've been assured that the snake most likely crawled into the tub by itself. There's nothing to worry about."

"'Most likely'?" Gregory snorted. "*That's* reassuring."

"You know, I have to admit this weekend is turning out to be much more exciting than I imagined," Sadie said, her eyes bright.

Joyce nodded.

Kenneth merely smiled. Julie had the feeling that he would have voiced his agreement if he hadn't feared word would get back to his wife. Susan probably wouldn't like the fact that her snake scare was a source of entertainment for her husband.

"Since everyone's together, let's get a snack and start quilting. Who's with me?" Julie asked, trying to sound as enthusiastic as possible. Not surprisingly, the responses she received were weak at best.

"Oh sure," Gregory said. "I relish the thought of quilting with a group of murder suspects."

"Do you think we should do that, dear? What with Susan still asleep upstairs?" Sadie's forehead was pinched with concern.

"We wouldn't want her to feel left out," Joyce added.

"She'll be fine," Kenneth said. "A little nap and she'll be right as rain."

Julie hated to admit it, but that was probably the best thing.

Carrie gave a lukewarm shrug of agreement.

Liam simply whistled and rolled up his sleeves.

A wild pop song suddenly blared from Sadie's purse.

"Ah!" Carrie nearly jumped out of her seat. She quickly recovered and looked down at her hands.

Sadie peeked at her phone. "Another sales call. Sometimes I answer just to toy with them. Tell them I'm going to buy everything then pretend to have a heart attack and hang up. But this is much more entertaining." She silenced the ringer. "Not a fan of CeCe's music, dear?" Sadie looked at Carrie.

"Um, it's fine," Carrie said, turning two shades of red. "It just startled me."

With Shirley's help, they pushed the tables to the outside edges of the room. Hannah had already explained to Julie how the Amish held their quilting frolics. She'd spent a lot of time living near the Amish in Pennsylvania before she joined Julie in the art retrieval world.

The theory was simple; most of the blocks were pieced in advance. Once everyone got together, they sewed the blocks together to make the quilt top. Then they made a "quilt sandwich" with batting in between the top and a white backing fabric. They placed it in a large frame so they could all sit around the frame to quilt the layers together. According to Hannah, this was the perfect gossip time for the Amish women.

Everyone pulled up a chair and threaded their needles. All except for Kenneth. His wife was the quilter in the family. He'd come along strictly for her.

"What did everyone do today?" Julie asked in an attempt to jump-start the conversation.

"Susan and I went to the winery," Kenneth said.

"Which one?" Julie asked.

He shrugged. "One with good wine."

"Sadie and I toured a few historic homes," Joyce said.

"That sounds like fun," Julie said automatically. The conversations at the inn were often as vanilla as they came, but at least they weren't talking about murders and snakes. "What about you, Carrie? What did you do?"

"Walked around town a bit, I guess." The girl pushed her owl-like glasses a little further up onto the bridge of her nose and squinted at Julie.

"How long are we going to do this?" Gregory asked. He had taken up his needle and thread. Though his fingers looked clumsy and awkward, his stitches were carefully executed.

"A couple of hours," Julie said, tamping down her impatience. "Then you can get ready for dinner."

Gregory shook his head. "I don't mean quilt. Pretend that nothing happened."

"We're not pretending," Liam interjected. "We're just making the best of a lousy situation."

"Well, I for one think this is ludicrous," Gregory said.

"If you're not up for quilting," Julie said, "why not relax in the library or take in some of the town until dinner is served?"

"I'm going to my room," Gregory said. Then he stood with a flourish and pushed his chair back under the frame a little too forcefully. "Can't say I'm looking forward to another dinner in this place." With a sardonic bow, he pulled the poker out of the fire tool set next to the fireplace in the tearoom and made his way to the door. "Just in case the killer gets any ideas," he called over his shoulder, waving the fire poker.

With his departure, some of the tension in Julie's shoulders seemed to leave as well. She glanced around at the remainder of her guests, heads all bent over their work. That was when it caught her eye. She hadn't noticed until that very moment that Gregory wasn't the only one who was "armed." All of her guests appeared to have makeshift weapons.

Sadie had a knife—a really large knife—sticking out of her purse. Since Sadie and Joyce were rarely seen apart, Julie could only assume they intended to share it.

Liam had a small baseball bat stuck between his belt and waistband like a sword. It was only about eighteen inches long, similar to the kind she'd seen given away as promotions. But Julie supposed it could inflict bodily harm in a pinch.

Kenneth had a can of mega-hold hairspray on his lap.

Whatever Carrie had, she wasn't revealing it. But Julie thought she had the *look* of someone with a concealed weapon. As she studied Carrie, Hannah's voice popped into her head and admonished her for letting her imagination run wild. Julie sighed and decided she'd better just address the facts.

"Sadie, I—"

"Yes, dear?" The older lady looked up and met Julie's gaze, her expression innocent and oddly cheerful.

"I'm not sure it's appropriate for you to be carrying that knife around the inn. It's very large … and sharp." Julie resisted the urge to use the term "small machete" to describe it.

Sadie smiled and then turned her attention back to the quilt block in front of her. "Oh, given the current circumstances, I think it's more than appropriate."

Julie tried again. "I understand the need to feel safe. But

there are better ways. Pepper spray, perhaps?"

"I don't think so, dear. I like my chances with this knife much better."

"Sadie, I'm sorry, but I cannot allow you to openly carry a weapon like that around the inn. What if you accidentally cut your hand? Or someone else's hand?"

Sadie looked up again, all wide-eyed innocence. "You want me to put it all the way in my handbag?" She lifted the large white bag and tucked the knife deeper inside.

"I'm afraid not." Julie held out her hand, palm up. "If I'm not mistaken, that's from our kitchen."

"But there's a murderer staying here." Sadie whispered the words as if everyone in the room didn't already know the dark secret.

"I really must insist."

Sadie looked as if she might protest further, but then her mouth twisted into a disapproving pucker, and she placed the handle of the knife in Julie's hand.

Joyce leaned over and whispered something in Sadie's ear. The smaller woman nodded and patted her handbag. Julie could only imagine what other kitchen utensils were hidden inside.

"Thank you," Julie said. Then she switched her focus to Liam. "Dr. Preston, what did you do today?"

The man everyone knew as Liam Preston didn't answer. His head remained bent over his work.

"Dr. Preston?" Julie asked again, wondering what he would do if she called him L.P.

His head jerked up. "Yes? Oh, sorry about that. What did you say?"

"I asked what you did this afternoon."

"I went to the library."

Kenneth raised his teacup in salute. "Here's to living life on the edge."

Liam shot him an irritated look.

"Can I join in?" Shirley didn't wait for an answer but pulled out the chair Gregory had recently vacated.

Julie smiled as Shirley started doing what Shirley did best—entertain.

"How about I tell you all a little story," Shirley said.

Kenneth had been slouched in his chair, but his eyes perked up at Shirley's suggestion. Of all of them, he had to be the most bored. He wasn't a quilter.

"Enjoy, everyone," Julie said, standing and brushing the wrinkles from her slacks. "I have a few things to do before dinner." *Like return the sword Sadie swiped from the kitchen.*

Julie paused outside the door, glancing back at the guests as they quilted and listened to Shirley's story. She couldn't figure out who seemed to be having the hardest time with their stitching, Joyce or Carrie. She finally decided on Carrie. The poor girl's face was practically pressed to the fabric as she laboriously executed each stitch. Evidently, the young woman needed a new prescription for her glasses. The one she was using now clearly was not cutting it.

Joyce made a stitch or two and then found something else to do with her hands. She'd get a drink of water and then pat her hair back into place. She laid her hand on Sadie's arm as they talked. For whatever reason, her concentration seemed to be split between the quilt and everything else going on around her.

But what did any of it mean? Both behaviors were odd. But did they point to a possible killer?

SIX

The bell over the door chimed. Julie turned, wondering where they were going to put this next round of spectators, but smiled as she recognized the visitor.

Daniel smiled in return. "I came by to see how you're holding up."

"I'm up," Julie said. "We were something of a tourist destination spot today, but it finally slowed down."

"People came to see the police tape?" Daniel asked, incredulous.

"And drive my staff crazy. Even Inga complained this afternoon."

"Inga?" His brows shot up in surprise.

"Shirley too."

"Shirley I can understand, but Inga?"

Julie nodded. "I know. She's usually so stoic under pressure."

"I was hoping you might have a minute to talk," Daniel said.

"I'm sure I can spare a minute or two." Talking to Daniel sounded like a welcome reprieve from her day.

Daniel flashed a satisfied grin. When he smiled like that, Julie wanted to promise him more than a few minutes.

She led the way back to her office.

"Detective Frost called me yesterday," Daniel said, taking a seat in front of her desk. "He asked me a few questions."

"Oh?"

"Standard stuff. Basically the same questions from the other night." Daniel pressed his fingertips together. "It almost felt like he was trying to trip me up."

"Figures," Julie said. "There's a real killer out there—maybe even staying here—and he wants to grill you." While Julie felt certain Everett Frost was a fine detective, she also knew he was as tenacious as a bulldog. She hoped he didn't spend too much time chasing a bad lead.

Daniel sat forward in his chair. "Do you honestly think one of your guests is a murderer?"

Julie threw her hands in the air with exasperation. "I don't know. I trust my staff, you know that. So, unless someone broke in, killed Alice Peyton, and then got out before we got the lights on, it has to be one of the guests."

"With an accomplice," Daniel said.

"How do you figure?" Julie asked.

"Someone flipped the breaker."

"Or it was a coincidence that someone took advantage of," Julie said.

"Or Alice Peyton got up, tripped, and hit her head," Daniel said.

"It seems about as far-fetched as one of the guests doing it," Julie said.

"Have you checked them out?"

She simply smiled.

"Dumb question. What have you found out?"

"I wish I could tell you that I have some great leads, but everyone checks out to be who they said. Well, mostly."

"What do you mean, 'mostly'?"

She explained how Carrie didn't show up in any of her searches and that Liam Preston was actually L.P. Wallis, famous mystery author.

Daniel snapped his fingers. "I *knew* that guy looked familiar."

"Well, don't bring any books into the inn to be auto-graphed. I'm keeping that bit of information under wraps for now. There has to be a reason why he doesn't want anyone to know who he is."

"He probably wants a break from fans asking for autographs," Daniel said, looking a little disappointed.

"Then there was the issue with the snake." She recounted that incident.

"Do you think someone planted it there?"

"I can't rule out the possibility. I mean, there are only two bathrooms on that floor. Any one of the guests could have done it. Even Carrie." Even though the girl was staying in the tower suite, the tiny blonde had just as much access to that bathroom as any of the other guests.

"Well, this certainly puts a new spin on things," Daniel said.

Julie blew a wayward curl of dark hair out of her face. "I just wish Millie were here. This whole weekend was her idea, and it's been one disaster after another. I emailed her the day I found the Civil War book and still haven't heard back."

"Were you able to get someone to come look at the book?" Daniel asked.

"I talked to a guy Friday morning. He said it didn't sound like anything he would want to see. Basically, Civil War journals and such are worth a lot if they can be traced back to a famous person or even a regular Joe who fought in a pivotal battle. As far as I can tell, I don't have that."

Daniel frowned. "So it's not worth anything?"

"The guy said it would be worth about two to three hundred dollars at most. But here's the weird thing—Alice worked for him."

"Alice? The *victim* Alice?"

"The very same."

"Coincidence?" Daniel asked.

Julie shrugged.

"I have to admit," Daniel said, "I'm a little sad that it's not worth more."

Always the historian.

"If it *was* worth more," Julie said, "I'd be back in the basement, searching for something else to donate. Maybe Millie won't want to let it go, and I'll be back to the drawing board anyway. For all I know, it belonged to her great-great-grandfather or something."

"You have enough to worry about right now. The donation can slide," Daniel said in a clear effort to calm her.

"A guest died during my watch," Julie said with a little more emotion than she expected. "I will *not* disappoint the elementary school fundraisers."

Daniel looked like he wanted to jump up and hug her, but Julie waved her hand to indicate she was OK. "It's just been a frustrating weekend—all of us packed in here."

"Have the police given you any idea about when they'll release the scene?" Daniel asked. "That'll help."

"No," Julie said with a shake of her head. "A few officers were in and out today, but it was chaos here. I didn't get to talk to them. I have no idea what kind of progress they've made, if any."

A knock sounded on the door. "Julie?"

"Come in, Hannah."

Her petite assistant opened the door and stepped inside. "Oh. Hi, Daniel."

Julie was struck by how much Hannah and Carrie Windsor resembled each other with their elfin features and glasses—although Carrie blended in with the wallpaper every chance she got, and Hannah somehow stood out no matter how much she tried not to.

"Is something wrong?" Julie asked.

Hannah sighed. "Shirley suggested that I make simpler

treats for the tearoom. She said these gawkers are a bit ... different. She thinks something more workaday would make us more money."

"'Workaday'?" Daniel echoed.

Hannah glanced at him. "You know. Ordinary."

"Sure." He chuckled. "I've just never heard the term used to describe tearoom snacks."

Hannah turned back toward Julie. "Shirley suggested sugar cookies. With *frosting*." She made it sound as if the mere mention would poison anyone within in a three-mile radius.

"I was thinking chocolate chip cookies," Julie said. "Everyone likes those."

"Or marshmallow treats," Daniel said.

Julie saw the twinkle in his eye as he made Hannah squirm.

"Oh, yeah. Those are the best," Julie chimed in. "With rainbow sprinkles mixed in."

"I've worked hard for the past six months to bring a certain standard of baking to the tearoom," Hannah said, clearly barely containing her indignation. "Sugar cookies and rainbow sprinkles would undermine everything I've built."

Julie and Daniel both broke into laughter.

"You were kidding me?" Hannah asked.

Julie answered with a nod as she continued to laugh.

"OK, you were kidding me." Hannah cracked a smile as she recovered her composure. "Not nice." She looked between them, settling her mock glare on Daniel. "You started it. You're a bad influence."

"Hey, I'm just glad she laughed about something." He held up his hands in surrender. "You ladies are tense."

Julie sat back in her seat and collected herself. "The kitchen is your domain. I bow to your expertise."

Hannah beamed. "Thank you. I could just picture the

horrified look on Millie's face if she came in and we were serving ..." She shook her head.

Yeah, there was that. Millie expected them to maintain high standards. Selling the same fare as the grocery store bakery would never cut it.

"Will you talk to Shirley about it?" Hannah asked. "I mean, I think it would be better coming from you."

Julie nodded. "Of course."

"Thanks." Hannah opened the door and stepped into the hallway just as Inga pushed past her and entered the office.

"What is this?" Inga demanded with a scowl. She held up a small space heater and a timer. "And what is it doing shoved underneath the armoire in the front room?"

"You found that in the sitting room?" Julie asked.

"When I was vacuuming. It's junky, and it collects dust."

Julie furrowed her brows. "I have no idea. I certainly didn't put it there."

"Let me see that," Daniel said, reaching for the heater. He examined it, poking at a wayward wire that stuck out from the bottom. "You found it plugged into that timer?"

Inga nodded and dropped the timer onto the desk like it had the plague. "Waste of energy. No one needs a heater this time of year."

Daniel quirked a brow. "They do if they're trying to blow a fuse at a certain time. Looks like it's been tampered with to increase the amps that it draws. It would only need to click on for a moment to trip the main breaker."

Julie nodded slowly, his meaning sinking in. "That's it. This solves the mystery of why the lights went out earlier than planned. The question is, who did it?"

Inga harrumphed. "Someone with absolutely no common sense."

Julie opened her mouth to respond, but the sounds of angry shouts floated into the office and cut her off.

"What now?" she asked, jumping out of her seat.

SEVEN

This is what I get for taking a break, Julie thought, hurrying to the tearoom.

The yelling continued as she and Daniel entered the room. He let out a shrill whistle. Everyone fell silent.

Julie scanned the faces of her weekend guests. They seemed to have grouped themselves into factions. Gregory and Kenneth stood toe to toe. Susan hovered behind her husband. Carrie lingered off to one side next to Joyce and Sadie, while Liam remained seated. It was a clear picture of "us versus them," with Gregory being "us" and everyone else being "them." When had he come back downstairs?

"Would someone please tell me what's going on in here?" Julie asked, looking at each one of them in turn. It was apparently a bad choice of phrasing, for no one moved. "OK then." She glanced around again. "Sadie," she said. The older woman jumped. "Why was everyone yelling?"

Sadie cast a suspicious eye at Gregory and then patted her big white purse with a wrinkled hand. "I don't know the whole story, dear," she started, her fingers on her bag and her gaze still glued to the big man. "But it seems that Gregory here accused Kenneth of cheating at checkers."

"That's right," Gregory said. "I did."

"Who cheats at *checkers*?" Daniel asked.

"Exactly," Kenneth muttered through clenched teeth as he continued to glare at the other man.

"My point as well." Gregory narrowed his eyes at Kenneth. "If a man will cheat at checkers, what else is he capable of?"

"Are you actually suggesting that *Kenneth* had something

to do with the murder?" Susan's voice was shrill with disbelief.

Gregory raised one brow. "Why should he be above suspicion? Because he plays with feet all day?"

Kenneth started toward him, but Daniel pulled him back. In an instant, Liam was on his feet, restraining Gregory.

Julie shot Daniel a grateful look. He gave her a tiny nod and then urged Kenneth across the room.

"Come with me," she said to Gregory, leading him away. As they headed across the room, she noticed that he still held the fire poker in his hand. "And give me that." She wrested the tool from his hand as they moved to a table away from the others.

He sat down with his back to the wall, and she supposed she couldn't find fault with his choice. Everyone was walking on pins and needles. Julie joined him at the table, hoping to defuse his anger, but not confident that she was the right person for the job.

"Would you like to tell me what happened?" Julie asked.

"No."

"Tell me anyway."

Gregory sighed with a whistly sound that seemed to expel a great deal of his tension. "That guy," he said with a nod toward Kenneth.

"What about him?" she asked. "He seems nice enough."

"A little *too* nice, don't you think? He came in grumpy that first day, but since Alice died, he's been nothing but smiles."

"That doesn't mean he's guilty of murder," she said.

"I suppose not, but ..." He looked out toward the front of the inn.

"But what?"

Gregory turned back to stare at his hands as they rested on the table. "I wasn't going to say anything, but the night of the murder, I heard a man and a woman talking. And they did not sound happy."

Julie tried to ignore the prickle at the base of her spine, but it was there all the same. "When was this?"

"Before dinner," Gregory said. "I was in my room, getting ready, and I heard voices outside."

"What were they saying?"

"Something about a book—or maybe it was books." He shrugged. "I don't know, like accounting or something."

Books. And Alice worked for Eric Rutherford, book expert. Coincidence or setup? "Did you recognize their voices?"

Gregory shook his head. "But when I looked outside, I saw her. It was Alice Peyton, all right."

"And you think she was talking to Kenneth?"

"I know she was."

"You saw him too, then?"

"No, but I saw a man reach out and grab her arm. I could just see his sleeve. That blue revolutionary jacket he had on was distinctive, wouldn't you say?"

Absolutely.

Julie sat back, her mind scrambling to process the implication.

"Here's the other thing," Gregory added. "Kenneth was sitting next to Alice at dinner. He was the closest person to Alice just before she died."

"So, how did this all start, exactly?" Julie asked Shirley after everyone had vacated the room, leaving only the two of them and Daniel in the tearoom.

"That Gregory Wilson." Shirley frowned. "He started

accusing everyone of all sorts of things. Evidently, he spent his afternoon doodling everyone."

"Doodling?" Julie asked.

"You know, on the computer."

"Oh. *Googling.*" Julie hid her smile.

"He said that Kenneth is spending all his money putting his kids through college. As if that's some kind of crime."

"I wonder if that's why Susan looks so ... forlorn," Julie said. It was the nicest word she could think of to describe the woman. Susan had lost all the sparkle she had when she arrived at the inn on Friday afternoon.

"It's sad," Shirley whispered. "Her nerves are clearly shot."

"Anything else of note?"

Shirley shrugged, her crystal earrings glittering in the lights. "Nothing really. Once the shouting started, I couldn't make out much detail."

"Thanks, Shirley. Keep your eyes open, OK? Let me know if you see anything suspicious."

The redhead nodded. "I will."

Julie watched the woman walk away and then turned back to Daniel. "How did it go with Kenneth?"

Daniel rubbed the back of his neck. "It went strangely."

"What do you mean?" She indicated the table closest to them and pulled out a chair. It sounded like she might need to get comfortable for this.

He settled into a chair and propped one ankle over the opposite knee. "Just that. Strange. Kenneth said they were all down here, playing checkers and quilting, when Gregory returned wielding his fire poker."

Julie eyed the poker that now lay across the chair to her right.

"According to Kenneth," Daniel continued, "Gregory

accused him of cheating. Gregory also claimed to have seen him Friday night."

Julie nodded. "Gregory told me he saw Kenneth and Alice talking Friday before dinner."

"Kenneth swears up and down it's a lie, and that he never set eyes on Alice before that night."

"Did Kenneth say this in front of his wife?" Julie asked.

Daniel's gaze jerked to hers. "Are you suggesting ...?"

Julie could only shrug. "Who can say? Obviously one of them is lying."

"And the only person who can tell us which story is true is dead," Daniel said.

"You got it."

At seven o'clock, Hannah announced that it was time to eat. The menu consisted of roasted lamb with red wine–and–garlic gravy, savory three-cheese potatoes, and asparagus tips. It was as extraordinary as ever. If Hannah kept cooking like this, they might have to start serving dinner to the general public.

Julie shook her head at the thought. That was just what she needed, more people to deal with. She had enough on her hands. She took a bite of lamb and surveyed her guests.

Kenneth had eaten every bit of his meal and was finishing up what was left of Susan's while Sadie and Joyce were gushing over the tenderness of the lamb.

Gregory, she noticed, ate everything he was given, soaking up the remainder of his gravy with the yeast rolls Hannah had baked. At least with his mouth full, he wasn't complaining.

Besides Joyce and Sadie, no one was making eye contact or even talking, but at least they weren't arguing and shouting.

"Julie." Hannah appeared at her side, the inn's phone in her hand. "There's a call for you. He asked for you by name."

"It's a he?" Shirley asked with a wink.

Julie waved away her insinuation and accepted the receiver from Hannah. Giving a nod to the others to excuse herself from the table, she walked out into the main lobby. "This is Julie."

"Julie Ellis?"

"Yes."

"My name is Aston Cooper. I'm the museum curator for the National Museum in Chicago."

Chicago? "What can I do for you, Mr. Cooper?"

"Aston, please." His voice was deep and confident. "I understand you have a Civil War journal in your possession."

"How do you know that?"

"Word gets around, Miss Ellis."

"Julie," she automatically corrected, meandering toward the front desk.

"I was hoping that I could schedule a time to look at the book. That is, if it's still for sale," Aston said.

"Unfortunately, I can't answer that. I'm waiting on word from the owner to see if it's OK to add it to the school auction."

"Would you mind if I take a look at it before then?" His voice carried an urgent edge.

"No, but I've already contacted a book expert and was told that it's worth no more than three hundred dollars. It might be a wasted trip for you."

"I would like to see for myself."

Is this some sort of hoax? Julie couldn't help but wonder. Aston Cooper didn't sound like any museum curator she'd ever talked to, and in her former life, she'd talked to many. This man sounded more like a radio host or an announcer for a car commercial than a lover of all things old.

"May I ask the name of the book expert you contacted?" he continued.

"Eric Rutherford."

Aston groaned.

"I take it you don't think very highly of him?" Julie asked.

"Yes. Let's leave it at that."

A crash sounded from the breakfast-now-dinner area. Julie turned her attention to the doorway and glanced in at her guests, half expecting to see Gregory wielding some new weapon while Sadie held him at knifepoint. But it appeared that Carrie had only knocked her water goblet to the floor.

"So, may I view the book? Miss Ellis?"

"Uh, sure," Julie said. "I suppose that would be fine."

"Excellent. One more thing," Aston said. "Would you be willing to scan a few of the pages into your computer and email them to me?"

"I have a couple of pictures digitized already. Will that be sufficient?"

"I'd love to see them. But what I'm most interested in is the copyright page, the title page and any back matter. Here's my email address." He rattled off the address, and Julie jotted it down on a piece of scrap paper.

"I won't be able to do this until first thing in the morning," she warned.

"That'll be fine. As long as you promise not to sell it to anyone else before I can see it."

"It's a deal," Julie said, wondering why now all of a sudden everyone seemed so interested in the book. Yesterday it hadn't been worth more than a couple hundred dollars. Now she had a curator calling from Chicago?

Word gets around. That's what he'd said. Though she wasn't exactly sure what he meant by that.

"Julie! Oh Julie, dear."

She turned to see Sadie approaching at a surprisingly quick pace, her big white handbag tucked close to her body. Joyce was nowhere to be seen.

"Hi, Sadie. Is everything all right?"

After a very tense dinner, everyone had gone their separate ways. Kenneth and Susan had left the inn to go for a walk, Gregory had hurried up to his room, and Sadie and Joyce had gone out to enjoy the garden. Liam and Carrie … she had no idea where they'd gone.

"Do you have a minute, dear?" Sadie asked.

"Of course."

Sadie clutched her handbag tight against her midriff and looked from one side to the other as if checking to see if they were truly alone. "I thought you should know," Sadie started in a loud whisper, "I saw that handsome Liam Preston down here, poking around after everyone had gone to bed last night."

And what were you *doing down here?* The question was on the tip of Julie's tongue, but she managed to bite it back. "What was he doing?"

Sadie's gaze skittered around the room again. "Nosing around like he was looking for something."

"Maybe he dropped his cellphone or his room key."

"Or maybe he was looking for the murder weapon."

"Sadie, the police have the murder weapon. It was the candlestick, remember?"

"Or maybe that's what the murderer wants you to think."

"I see." What else could she say?

"You know he's not who he says he is." Sadie glanced around again. "He's really that famous mystery writer, L.P. Wallis."

"Yes, I know," Julie said, waiting to see where this might lead.

"What if all this was for research?"

Julie blinked. "I beg your pardon?"

"Research, you know." She leaned in closer. "He writes about murders all the time."

"You think he killed Alice to get information for his next book?"

"I'm sad to say it, but yes. The thought did cross my mind."

With tremendous willpower, Julie resisted the urge to laugh. She didn't want to offend the sweet old lady, but of all the possible scenarios, this wasn't one that held much promise. "Thank you, Sadie."

"You're welcome, dear. Since you run the inn, I thought you should be the first to know. Tomorrow, I'm going to the police station to tell that handsome Detective Frost what I discovered."

"I'm sure he'll appreciate that." This time Julie couldn't hide her smile.

EIGHT

Sunday-morning breakfast went more smoothly than Julie could have hoped. Whether it was this morning's Amish-style baked oatmeal or the previous night's dessert, something had taken the frown from Gregory's face. He seemed almost pleasant.

Julie wasn't about to ask him why. She just thanked the heavens for small favors and finished up her own meal. So far there had been no murders, no snakes, and no brawls over board games. The morning had started on a decidedly positive note.

"You're looking well today, Susan," Julie said. Since last night's dinner, the woman seemed to have pulled herself together. Perhaps the evening walk had done her some good.

"We're going to church this morning," Kenneth supplied.

"Me too," Carrie chimed in.

Julie was certain this was the first information the petite blonde had offered freely.

"That sounds like a wonderful idea," Sadie said. "Joyce?"

"Let's do it." The other woman smiled.

Gregory stood, and Julie was dismayed to see his usual frown had returned.

"Will you be joining us for Sunday worship, Mr. Wilson?" Sadie asked, her blue eyes bright.

"With the likes of you people? I think not." He gave them all the stink eye and then stalked from the room. Julie could hear his heavy footsteps on the stairs as he ascended.

"Well," Joyce huffed.

"What about you, Dr. Preston?" Susan asked.

Liam snapped to attention. "I have some, uh, things to do here. Sorry, ladies." He rose from his seat and hustled out of the room as if the devil were on his heels.

"Will you join us, Miss Ellis?" Sadie's voice was sweet and hopeful.

"I'm afraid I have to decline as well." With all the craziness going on at the inn, she didn't dare leave for a minute. Once the weekend was over, she planned to get out. But for now, she was staying put.

"Your loss," Joyce shrugged, and together the two friends stood. They waited for Carrie, Kenneth, and Susan. Then the five of them left the inn together.

Julie poured herself another cup of coffee and headed toward her office. She still had to take the pictures of the journal's pages and email them to Aston Cooper.

With any luck, this morning would be a lot smoother than the previous one. If there were too many more interruptions, she would be so far behind, Millie would have no choice but to come back.

Speak of the devil, Julie thought a few minutes later when she opened her email. A note from Millie was second from the top under an email from that poor Nigerian prince who hadn't found anyone to take his money yet. She sent that one to the junk file and opened Millie's.

Having a wonderful time in Baja. It is so beautiful here. The water looks like aquamarine and diamonds. Do whatever you want with the book. I don't even know where it came from. It's probably been in the basement since it was written.

Hope the murder mystery weekend is going fabulous. Can't wait to hear all about it when I return.

Toodles—M

Well, at least she had her answer about the journal.

Julie looked up from the computer screen as Hannah entered the room and settled herself into a chair.

"Breakfast was delicious," Julie said.

"Of course." Hannah was humble about most things, but not her culinary skills.

"What's on your mind?" Julie leaned back in her chair and pushed a curl out of her eyes.

"I don't know if I should even bring it up." Hannah frowned. "It's about Gregory."

"What about him?"

"I saw him sneaking around down here last night after everyone had gone to their rooms. He seemed to be looking for something."

That sounded familiar. It seemed the paranoia was catching. "Maybe he dropped his phone or his favorite pen. He could have been looking for anything."

"I suppose, but it seemed really strange to me, you know?" Hannah stood. "I thought I should tell you."

"Thanks. I appreciate it."

"I've got to get back to the kitchen."

Julie nodded, but she felt like something else was amiss. Hannah turned to go.

"Are you sure everything's OK?" Julie asked.

Hannah sighed. "I'll just be glad when this weekend is over."

Julie couldn't agree more. Nine o'clock tomorrow night marked the seventy-two–hour deadline. The guests would all be free to leave town.

Which reminded her, she needed to contact Monday's guests to make sure they understood that the check-in time would be delayed until evening. She would let them know she could accept their luggage; she could tuck it away in the library until the rest of this weekend's guests had vacated their rooms. It was going to be a mess—no doubt about it. But once that was done, it would all be over, and she hoped everything in the Quilt Haus Inn would go back to normal. Fortunately, she only had two couples checking in on Monday.

She rose from her seat to retrieve the journal from the safe, but she was shocked to find the small vault empty.

Confused, she quickly retraced her steps from Friday night. *I did put it away, didn't I?*

Perhaps Daniel took it in all of the commotion, and she just didn't remember it.

She sighed. She was grasping at straws, but right now that was all she had. She picked up the phone and called Daniel's number.

"Franklin," he answered after the third ring.

"It's Julie."

"What a nice surprise." His voice came across the line deep and masculine. "Don't tell me something else has happened at the inn." When she didn't respond right away, he said, "Julie?"

"Did you by chance take the journal with you on Friday night?"

"The Civil War journal?"

"Yes."

"Why would I take it?"

She sighed. "I was afraid you were going to say that."

"It's missing?" he asked.

"It would seem so. I had a man call last night about it. He said he worked for a museum in Chicago."

"How did he know about it?"

Julie's mouth twisted into a frown. "He said 'Word gets around,' whatever that means. He wanted me to take some additional pictures of it and email them to him. But when I came into my office to get it, it was gone."

"From the safe?"

"That's the thing. With the murder and the police and everything on Friday night, I can't remember if I put it back in the safe. Do you remember?"

"I don't. Sorry."

"If I didn't put it in the safe, what could I have possibly done with it?" she mused.

"I wish I could tell you."

Julie leaned back in her chair, feeling deflated. "Me too."

Daniel offered to come over and help her search, but she declined. If it had been misplaced, she'd find it.

It wasn't under the papers piled on her desk. Or in any of the drawers. It wasn't buried in the recycle bin or mixed in with the stack of old newspaper crossword puzzles that she always kept but never managed to get around to working.

Before she knew it, two hours had passed, and there was still no Civil War journal. She pushed back from her desk and made her way to the kitchen.

As usual, Hannah was in the middle of baking something scrumptious, still neat as a pin as she did so.

"What's on today's menu?" Julie asked.

"These are sourdough rolls for tonight," Hannah explained. "I thought I'd get a jump on them so they have plenty of time to rise. Did you come to lend a hand?"

"You know you don't want me in the kitchen."

"Sadly, yes. So, what brings you in?"

Julie plucked a pear from the bowl of fruit on the counter and wiped it on a nearby towel. "I can't find the Civil War journal."

Hannah stopped kneading the dough and pushed her glasses up using the back of one gloved hand. "It's missing?"

Julie took a bite of the fruit and nodded as she chewed.

"Have you talked to Shirley? Maybe she's seen it. Or Inga."

Inga. "Good idea."

With her crepe-soled shoes and austere gray uniform, Inga was like a ghost in the inn. She cleaned things without anybody noticing she was there until the deed was done. Inga had to have seen it. Maybe the housekeeper didn't realize its significance and moved it back to the basement where Julie had found it. Or maybe she did recognize it, called the school, and had them come get it for the auction, not knowing that Julie had only this morning received the green light to donate from Millie. She was nothing if not efficient.

"Thanks, Hannah." Julie smiled at her friend and went in search of the elusive housekeeper. She found her on the third floor, changing the linens in Carrie's room.

"Inga, can I ask you something?"

The woman paused long enough for Julie to continue, but otherwise didn't answer.

"Have you come across a really old book recently?"

A deeper frown than usual marred her strong brow. "Yes. The library is full of them."

"This one would have been in my office. I haven't seen it since Friday, and I need it."

"I'm sorry. I cannot help you."

"Then can you do me a favor? As you're cleaning today, will you keep an eye out for it?" Julie gave a brief description.

"Of course."

Julie nodded her appreciation and turned to leave the room. But a feeling that something wasn't right made her stop. She swung her gaze around the room, taking in every detail.

One small bag sat in the room's only chair. There was no makeup bag filled with cosmetics or clothes hanging in the open closet. And there was nothing personal in the room. No favorite pillow or lucky charm. Nothing to indicate that the occupant owned anything other than the sparse contents of the one small bag.

Odd for a young twenty-something girl.

It was a long shot, but better than nothing. Julie pushed into the library and scanned the shelves for the missing journal.

She'd spent the better part of the morning and early afternoon searching for the confounded book, but it was as if the thing had simply disappeared.

Ridiculous. She tucked one strand of her dark hair behind her ear and ran a finger along the spines of the many books in the small library. Inga was right. A lot of them were old—really, really old—but not one of them was a Civil War journal from 1861.

No closer to finding the book than she had been hours earlier, she left the library and headed back to her office. There was only one thing left to do. With a sigh, she picked up the phone and called Detective Frost.

It was almost four when Frost let himself into the inn. Julie was waiting for him and the rest of the guests to arrive from their day of church and sightseeing.

Frost shook his head and shot her a small smile. "It's always something around here, huh?"

"It seems that way." She swallowed back her sigh.

The bell over the door chimed, and Susan and Kenneth Calhoun swept into the room. Susan looked even better than she had that morning. Church seemed to have done her a lot more good than a decent night's sleep.

"I've had a wonderful day," Susan gushed.

Julie smiled in return. "I'm glad to hear that."

"And not once did I think about that mean old snake." Susan gave a wobbly smile.

"Snake?" Frost turned his dark gaze to Julie.

She nodded. Evidently, Susan wasn't over her shock as much as she pretended to be. Was her sunny disposition a ruse to keep suspicion off her husband?

Kenneth led Susan across the foyer and up the stairs. Julie couldn't help but view the pair with different eyes. *Had* Kenneth known Alice before they met on Friday night?

"You going to tell me about this snake?" Frost pinned her with a look.

Julie merely shrugged. There wasn't much to tell, but before she had the chance, the bell chimed again.

Sadie and Joyce entered, chattering like magpies.

"Just a moment." Julie excused herself and went to fetch Shirley. "Can you help me please?" she asked the redhead.

Shirley looked up from her book, *A Short History of Missouri*. The tome was about four inches thick. Little wonder that Shirley knew so much local lore; Julie had seen dictionaries with fewer pages.

"Of course," Shirley said. "What do you need?"

"Everyone is starting to get ready for the quilting. And Detective Frost is here."

"About the book?"

Julie nodded.

"I just can't imagine where it got off to." Shirley shook her head.

"Me neither. But I don't want to talk about it in front of the guests."

"Good plan. You go talk to the detective, and I'll hold down the fort," Shirley said.

Julie smiled. "Thanks."

As they went back to the front, Carrie stepped inside.

"Hi, Carrie," Shirley chirped. "Did you have a good day?"

"I did," the girl answered timidly.

"What did *you* do this morning?" the detective asked.

Carrie turned as pink as the hanging basket of petunias on the front porch. "I went to church and then did some shopping."

"It doesn't look like you bought much," Frost said. It was an understatement if ever there was one. Carrie had no bags to speak of, just a slouchy purse slung across her small frame.

"I window-shopped," she said before hurrying into the tearoom, bumping into the doorframe on her way in.

The detective caught Julie's gaze and arched his brows.

Yes, she knew it was strange to shop all afternoon long and not buy a single thing. And it was even weirder to say you were from one place and there be no record of you living there.

Yet just because Julie couldn't find out anything about the shy girl didn't mean she had taken the journal or that she had killed Alice. But one thing was certain—the petite blonde was hiding something.

NINE

"Where was the book when it disappeared?" Frost asked as they entered Julie's office.

"Locked in the safe." Julie paused. "I think."

"Think?"

"It's been a long couple of days." Julie tapped a finger to her chin. "I had just shown it to the guests—"

"All of them?"

She nodded.

"Together or one at a time?" he asked.

"Together. It was after everyone arrived."

He took out his notepad and made a few notations as Julie filled him in on the details.

"The article that appeared in our local paper was picked up by a larger publication," she said. "Word got around that we'd found a Civil War journal here at the inn, and they asked to see it."

"You're saying that your guests came here knowing you had the journal?"

"Yes." She didn't want to believe that any of her guests were capable of stealing the journal, but the fact remained that someone had. Was it the same person that killed Alice Peyton? Or did she have *two* criminals under her roof? "Or at least some of them did."

"Who?"

Julie thought back. "Sadie and Joyce knew about it. And Alice."

"Our murder victim?"

"The same."

"Anyone else?"

"I guess they were the only ones. At least they were the only ones who had said anything at the time."

"I see." Frost scribbled something on the notepad and then turned his sharp focus back to her. "You brought out the journal for everyone to see. Then what happened?"

"I brought it back in here and put it in the safe. ... I'm almost positive."

"And this was before Ms. Peyton was murdered."

"Yes."

The detective walked to the safe, studying it from a variety of angles. "Could you have put the book away and then accidentally set it on a day lock? Or perhaps not even locked it at all?"

"Unfortunately, that's very possible," Julie said.

"Did you unlock the safe when you discovered it was missing?"

"Yes," Julie said. "Then I searched the whole house for it."

"We could dust for latent prints, but the possibility of getting a clear print that isn't yours would be a long shot."

"Right," she muttered with irritation, even though she knew it wasn't the detective's fault.

"Has anyone staying here shown an exaggerated interest in the book?" Frost asked.

Sadie and Joyce had been eager to see the book, but Sadie was a retired librarian, and Joyce seemed to follow her lead on most everything. Liam had seemed very interested as well, but given the facts that he was a writer and a professor of literature, that would only be normal. Kenneth, Susan, and Carrie had shown average curiosity, while Alice and Gregory hadn't given it a second glance.

"Wait a minute," Julie said, pausing to get her thoughts in better order. "Even the average Joe would find something old and rare a little fascinating."

"Beg your pardon?"

"Alice and Gregory," she said. "Neither one of them even *looked* at the book."

"And you think that's strange?"

"Well, yeah," Julie replied. "I think most people would be at least a little interested in a Civil War journal from 1861."

"Noted," Detective Frost said. "Anything else?"

"I'm not sure if this matters or not, but Gregory was arrested for stealing a rare baseball card."

"When was this?" he asked. "When was he arrested?"

Julie shrugged. "A couple of years ago."

"And he came right out and told you this?"

"I searched it online," Julie admitted.

"What about Alice Peyton? Did you find out anything unusual about her?"

"Yeah," she said. "I did. Alice worked for Eric Rutherford, the first book expert I called about the journal. Now Alice is dead, and the journal is missing."

"Hmmm ..." Detective Frost wrote something in his small notebook.

"I'm wondering if the crimes are related."

"It's possible, but hard to know for sure. I hate to say it, but so far our investigation has turned up nothing in the way of concrete evidence that would point to any one person being responsible for Ms. Peyton's death."

Julie nodded. Not exactly comforting news.

"There's one other thing," she said. "We found a snake in one of the bathtubs yesterday."

"Is this the same snake Mrs. Calhoun mentioned earlier?" Frost asked.

"Yes," Julie said, feeling very much like a kid called before the principal for telling lies.

He frowned. "Why didn't you call me then?"

"The wildlife removal expert seemed to believe that it was a chance occurrence. He said the snake most likely crawled up a pipe."

"Was the snake venomous?" Frost asked.

"No."

"Hmmm …," the detective said again.

"It seemed like a perfectly logical explanation at the time," she added.

"But you think it's suspicious now?" He eyed her over the top of his notepad.

"I don't know. I'm starting to think *everything* is suspicious."

"Crime will do that to you." The detective's mouth twisted into a wry smile.

Lovely.

He made a couple more notes in his little book and then clicked his pen and tucked the tablet back into his pocket. "I'd like to talk to the guests. Find out if anyone saw anything that might shed some light on this."

"Of course."

Julie led the way back to the tearoom, where everyone had gathered. As promised, Shirley was playing hostess. The guests were seated around the frame, quilting and listening to Shirley spin another of her fantastic tales about the rich history of Straussberg. Julie wondered if everyone was quiet because she was telling a story or if she was telling a story because everyone was quiet.

"Did you find out who killed poor Alice?" Susan asked, her eyes darting anxiously around at the group.

"We're still investigating that, ma'am. Tonight I'm here for another matter. It seems that a very valuable book is missing, and I need to talk to you all about it."

"What's this?" Gregory grumped, looking up from his tiny stitches. "Now you're accusing us of theft?"

And so it begins.

"No one is accusing you of anything," Julie said calmly. "But the detective needs to know if anyone has seen anything suspicious recently."

"Besides a dead body in the dining room and a black mamba in the bathtub?" Joyce asked.

"We've already established that it was a rat snake and not anything poisonous," Julie said.

"Venomous," Sadie corrected. "There's a difference."

Julie said nothing and kept her pleasant smile pasted firmly in place.

"Perhaps it would be helpful if you clarify exactly what you mean by 'suspicious,'" Liam said.

This from the mystery writer.

"If you saw someone lurking in the halls after everyone had gone to bed," Julie clarified. "Or saw someone where they weren't supposed to be. Basically, anything out of the ordinary."

"No matter how small," the detective added. "Whatever it is, I need to know about it."

Julie made a mental note to tell the detective in private what Gregory had said about Kenneth. She wasn't sure how much stock to put in it, but he needed to know—assuming Gregory hadn't already told him.

"This entire weekend is out of the ordinary," Gregory said with a scowl.

"At least it's turned out to be interesting," Kenneth countered. Then he immediately looked like he wished he could take back the statement.

His wife smacked his arm. "Kenneth! What a thing to say."

Carrie ducked her head over her work and didn't look up. Was she concentrating? Maybe hiding something? Or merely laughing at the Calhouns' antics?

Detective Frost gave his spiel about contacting him if anyone remembered anything. He handed out business cards as Julie paced.

Despite his stern request, no one said a word. Of course not. There was a murderer among them. Everyone was afraid to step forward, thinking they might be next. Yet Julie wondered how many of them would be on the phone with the detective before darkness fell.

Millie was not going to like this. Julie didn't like it much either. It was ironic, really. She'd left behind the intrigue and subterfuge of underground antiquities thieves to have a peaceful stay in small-town Missouri. So far, her time here had been anything but peaceful.

Gregory held the detective's card as if it were contaminated with bubonic plague.

"And one more thing," the detective said, "I feel I should remind everyone that a murder investigation is still underway."

As if they could forget. Though the yellow police tape was gone from the dining area, they were still eating every meal in the breakfast room.

One more day, Julie told herself. *Just one more day.*

"Everyone is required to remain in town for the full duration of the seventy-two hours. I'll come by tomorrow evening and release you when it's time for everyone to leave."

Dinner was a quiet affair—as most of the meals had become. There was no denying that the inn's first murder mystery weekend had turned out to be a disastrous affair. Julie thought it was a solid argument against ever hosting another one. But knowing the owner the way Julie did, she was sure Millie would do whatever she felt like doing. It was one of the reasons Julie both admired her and wanted to strangle her at the same time.

Rich tomato soup started their meal, followed by a fresh green salad. Then the main course: Amish-inspired oven-fried chicken. Hannah had outdone herself again. The chicken was crispy on the outside, not too greasy, and perfectly seasoned. On the inside, it was tender and juicy.

The guests seemed to think so as well. Even Gregory was more relaxed. It appeared that the way to his good side might be through his stomach.

"This is so delicious," Sadie said.

Joyce moaned in response.

It was good, but hardly *that* good. Julie glanced up to see Joyce close her eyes. OK, maybe it was to some people.

Julie looked back to her plate but then jerked up her head as Susan screamed.

"Oh my word! Joyce is dying!" Susan exclaimed. "The killer struck again!"

Joyce careened over, falling to the floor with a soft thud.

Kenneth was on his feet in a split second. He raced to Joyce's side, turning her and grabbing her wrist to check her pulse.

Susan screamed again.

Julie rushed over to Kenneth. "What's wrong with her?" She pulled her phone from her pocket and dialed 911.

He shook his head. "Her pulse is fast, and her breathing is shallow."

"Does anyone know CPR?" Liam asked.

Kenneth shot him a look.

"Right. You're a doctor. Sorry."

Julie relayed the information to the dispatcher, who promised to send an ambulance immediately. She hung up the phone and looked at the older woman. Her eyes were closed; she looked like she was asleep.

"Oh my," Sadie gasped, placing a hand over her mouth. "This is terrible."

Everyone hovered around, but Kenneth motioned them back. "Give her some room."

"Has she had a heart attack?" Carrie asked.

"It appears so, but I'm a podiatrist. And it's been a long time since med school."

"Wait!" Sadie grabbed Joyce's handbag and started rifling through the contents. "Joyce is allergic to peanuts. Maybe she accidentally ate one."

"Could this be anaphylactic shock?" Julie asked Kenneth. She was no doctor, but it really looked like a heart attack to her. And Joyce was no spring chicken. Plus, Hannah was the most careful person there was; if Joyce had a peanut allergy, she knew about it.

"Here." Sadie found the EpiPen and held it toward Kenneth. Her hand was shaking.

"I've never seen anaphylaxis look like this," he mused, his hand still on her pulse. "There's no swelling or rash of any kind."

"Please," Sadie said, tears in her eyes. "If you wait too long, she'll certainly die."

Kenneth hesitated but then took the pen and administered the shot into Joyce's thigh just as Hannah entered with a shocked look on her face.

"Were there peanuts in the meal?" Julie demanded.

"Of course not," Hannah offered. "Joyce is allergic."

Poison sprang to Julie's mind, and she pushed the thought away. She couldn't jump to conclusions. She *wouldn't*.

The bell rang from the front of the inn followed by heavy footsteps.

"The ambulance is here," Liam said from the doorway. "I'll direct them back."

Joyce's eyelids fluttered a bit, but for the most part, she was as still as the dead.

"Clear some room," the EMT ordered.

Everyone took a step back and then another as they started to work on Joyce.

Julie said a little prayer that the woman would be OK. For her sake, for Sadie's sake, and for Millie's sake. Two dead bodies in one weekend were more than anyone should have to face.

The EMTs loaded Joyce into the ambulance, and with Sadie riding along, rushed her to the hospital.

Even though dinner was barely half over, no one seemed willing to continue to eat. Whether they were upset about Joyce or afraid for themselves, Julie didn't ask. A poisoning would surely be the icing on the disaster weekend cake.

Susan went up to her room, dragging her husband reluctantly behind. Gregory started for the front door, mumbling about getting something decent to eat, and Liam headed for the stairs with the preoccupied look in his eyes that he often got. Only Carrie remained in the tearoom with Julie and Shirley.

"Would it be all right if I worked on the quilt a little more?" Carrie asked in her soft voice.

"I don't see why not," Julie replied. Everyone had their

own way of working through stress and bad times. If stitching helped Carrie, then Julie wasn't about to tell her she couldn't quilt. After all, that was the real driving force behind the Quilt Haus Inn.

Carrie smiled, and her entire face lit up. "Great. If you need me, that's where I'll be."

Suddenly there was something very familiar about her, but Julie couldn't pinpoint what it was. The girl's smile was similar to another that Julie had seen before.

She sighed. Maybe it was because Carrie reminded her so much of Hannah. Whatever it was, Julie couldn't shake the strong sense of déjà vu as she made her way into the kitchen.

She found Hannah sitting on one of the stools at the island, biting her lip as she thumbed through a large cookbook. Either she was looking for something, or she was exercising her page-turning muscles. *Flip, flip, flip.*

"How is she?" Hannah asked, eyes on the cookbook.

"She was stable when they took her."

"Do they know what caused her ... whatever it was that happened?"

Julie shook her head. "I think it was a heart attack. But we won't know much of anything until tomorrow."

Hannah nodded, her shoulders stiff with worry.

"So, you knew that Joyce was allergic to peanuts?"

"Of course," Hannah answered, pulling her eyes from the book. "There's a place for that kind of information on the registration form. Plus, I double-check with all of our guests before their arrival in case I need to do any special ordering."

Julie remembered that there was a place on the registration form about allergies and special requests. Hannah was just so competent that Julie had pretty much not given the food another thought since taking the innkeeper job.

"And nothing had peanuts in it tonight?"

Hannah frowned. "Of course not."

"I'm sorry. I'm only asking for when Detective Frost interrogates me." Julie looked around the kitchen to see if anything looked amiss. "I know I'm being paranoid here, but if there were peanuts in her food, and you didn't put them there—"

"Then someone is trying to kill off all our guests."

"Judging from how everyone stopped eating after the incident," Julie said, "I think that's what they all suspect."

"Too bad," Hannah said with a pointed look at the wet-bottom shoofly pies she had made to cap off the Amish-theme dinner.

"Have you noticed anything weird going on recently in the kitchen?" Julie asked.

"Just that Gregory guy poking around." Hannah made a face.

"But nothing in here? Nothing was moved or missing?"

"Things are always moved and missing."

"Oh?" Julie asked.

"Inga."

The one word was all the explanation Julie needed. "Right."

"Everything that's happened," Hannah said. "It's too much to be a coincidence. Don't you think?"

"Yes," Julie said. "Alice's death, the snake, the journal, and now this."

"Do you think someone is trying to put Millie out of business?"

"I'm not sure." Julie broke off a chunk of the crusty French bread sitting near Hannah's elbow. "But I knew this murder mystery weekend was a bad idea."

"That bread is for tomorrow's breakfast, you know."

Julie shot her an apologetic grin. "Sorry. I guess I'm turning into a nervous eater."

"Now *that* concerns me."

"That I'm eating?" Julie asked.

"No, that you're nervous."

And she would be until they got word back from the hospital that Joyce was OK. Julie hated the thought of the woman being seriously ill. And stories like this could break an inn's reputation. She couldn't imagine her guilt if the Quilt Haus Inn went down the tubes on her watch.

"Will you let me know when Sadie calls?" Hannah asked.

"Definitely. Thanks for the bread." Julie headed for the tearoom. If anyone had seen anything noteworthy, it would be Shirley.

TEN

Julie found Shirley straightening up the tearoom, preparing to close it for the evening. She helped the energetic redhead sweep the floor and wipe down all the tables. After all, she couldn't very well ask too many questions with Carrie sitting right there.

Finally, the young girl stood and stretched, stifling a yawn even though it was barely eight o'clock. "I guess I'd better be getting to bed."

"So early?" Shirley asked. "A young thing like you should be out kicking up her heels and having a good time."

Carrie smiled. She really was a pretty girl, once you took away the huge glasses and baggy, librarian-gone-wrong clothing. "Oh, I have those nights too. But tonight I want to read a little; then I'll hit the hay."

"What are you reading?" Julie asked. With any luck the girl would say, "The Civil War journal I stole from your office."

Carrie blushed. *"Romeo and Juliet."*

Not the answer Julie had expected. "Really?"

"I adore that story." Shirley sighed and then made a face. "Except for the end. It could have ended much better. All that death."

"Don't ruin it for me," Carrie said.

Julie blinked. *Is she serious? Who doesn't know how* Romeo and Juliet *ends?*

"I've read that play so many times," Shirley continued, the whimsical tone of her voice taking over.

"I read it in high school English class," Julie said. "I remember that the boys hated it."

"This is a first for me," Carrie admitted.

"Seriously?" Shirley gasped. "Oh, honey, you have been missing out."

"You didn't read it in school?" Julie asked.

Carrie shrugged. "I, um, was mostly homeschooled. My tutor … I mean, my *mother* didn't think it was something I needed to experience at the time."

"Well, you're reading it now, dear, and that's all that matters." Shirley patted the girl's arm reassuringly. "Never too late."

Carrie smiled. "I guess. Good night."

"Good night," Julie murmured, wondering more and more what the girl's true story was. Too many things about her didn't add up.

"What is it?" Shirley asked after Carrie had left the room. "You've been hovering all night, waiting to ask me something. So go ahead."

"Aside from the obvious," Julie said, "have you noticed anything unusual this weekend?"

"Define unusual."

Julie shrugged. "Strange behavior. Anyone sneaking around. Weird noises."

Shirley shook her head. "I'm seeing the same things you are, I suppose. Poor Susan is putting on a brave face but looks like she's about to have a nervous breakdown any minute. Kenneth is having the time of his life despite his wife's anxiety, and Liam locks himself in his room every chance he gets. I wonder what he does in there," she mused.

Julie wasn't ready to let Liam's secret slip. He seemed like an honest enough guy in spite of his little white lie about his name. She would keep his true identity a secret for now.

"Carrie seems sweet enough," Shirley continued. "Sadie and Joyce are both nice as pie."

"Dare I ask your thoughts on Gregory?"

Shirley pressed her lips together. "My mama always said if you couldn't say something kind about a body, don't say anything at all."

"But?"

"That man is cranky," Shirley said. "All the time."

Truer words were never spoken. But Shirley wasn't saying anything that Julie didn't already know.

"Just continue to keep an eye out for anything unusual, will you please?" Julie asked.

Shirley nodded, her hair glinting like molten lava beneath the ceiling lights. "You bet."

Julie left the tearoom and went straight to her office. She had a little time before bed to look for the journal again and possibly do a little more online research to find out something about Carrie.

Or maybe I should just corner the timid blonde and question her outright. Julie shook her head as Detective Frost's earlier words floated through her suspicious mind: "Crime will do that to you."

Julie flipped on the light in her office and gasped. Stunned, she stared at the mess before her.

The room had been ruthlessly ransacked. Books lay scattered all over the floor. Her desk drawers were pulled out, their contents dumped to the side like trash. Even her trash can had been dumped and its contents obviously rifled through.

She shivered. *Who could have done this? And when?*

Julie refused to believe it could be one of her staff. With the exception of Hannah, they had all been here long before she had. And Julie had known Hannah for years. No, it had to be one of the guests. But who? And when could they possibly have found the time?

Thinking about it more, Julie had to admit that it *had* been a distracting evening. Perhaps someone did it during the drama at dinner. The ambulance could have attracted someone from the outside. Regardless of the answer, one thing was certain: She had to call the police again.

Reluctantly, Julie picked up her phone and dialed the all-too-familiar non-emergency number.

Dispatch promised to send someone right out.

Julie hung up with a sigh. Her fingers itched to clean up the mess, but that would have to wait. The police needed to see the room in all of its chaotic glory.

"Holy cow!" Hannah exclaimed behind her. "What happened in here?"

"I can only assume someone was looking for something." Julie brushed past Hannah and walked the short distance down the hall to the library and peered inside.

Everything in the room appeared to be in proper order.

"That's quite a deduction," Hannah drawled.

Julie shot her an annoyed look as she headed back to her office. "I don't know what they could possibly be after. Everyone already knows that the journal is missing."

"Maybe whoever took it hid it in here and came back for it," Hannah suggested.

"Why would they tear everything apart trying to find it? They would know exactly where they put it."

"True," Hannah said. "Whoever did this either wanted something else or hadn't heard the book was stolen."

Julie nodded.

Shirley's voice drifted into the office as her footsteps drew closer. "Right this way, officer." She poked her head in the door. "Julie, did you call the pol—my stars! What happened in here?"

"That's what I'm hoping the police can help me figure out."

Shirley stepped sideways to let the uniformed officer squeeze by. "But are you OK, dear?"

"I'm fine, Shirley. Thanks."

"When did you discover the room in this state?" the officer asked. He was young—almost too young—with light brown hair and tawny eyes like a hawk's. Had it not been for those keen eyes, she might have turned him around on the spot and sent him back to his car.

Where are they getting these babies to investigate crimes?

"I came in here about fifteen minutes ago," she replied. "And this is what I found."

"What were you doing at the time?"

"Preparing to finish some work before I went to bed."

"I see." The officer wrote something in the little notebook he held—the same kind Detective Frost carried around. "What sort of work?"

Julie felt her patience slip a notch. This weekend had been nothing but drama from beginning to end. "The usual stuff."

She was waiting for him to ask her to explain that answer when an all-too-familiar voice sounded from the hall. "If you wanted to see me again, you didn't have to go to such lengths."

"Detective Frost." Julie forced a polite smile to her lips. "So nice to see you this evening. What's it been—four hours?"

Frost stepped into the office. "Anything missing?"

"I haven't checked. I didn't want to disturb any clues or fingerprints."

"Any idea who could have done this?" Frost scanned the room. Julie was sure he didn't miss a single detail.

"I don't think it was the same person who stole the journal."

"Really? And what makes you so sure of that?"

Julie shrugged. "Why would the thief do this if they already had the journal?"

"Hmmm. And there's nothing else of great importance in here?" He raised his eyebrows in that infuriating way he had.

"Accounting records, registration papers, that sort of thing."

"What about a checkbook or business credit cards?"

"That's all locked in the safe," Julie said.

Frost shot her a skeptical look.

"It's locked." She pointed to the closed door of the tiny wall vault. "May I?"

He fished in his pocket and then held out a pair of latex gloves to her.

Julie pulled the gloves on as she picked her way across the office, trying her best not to step on anything that looked important. These were Millie's paper records scattered across the floor, and she wanted to return them to their proper homes as soon as possible. And without footprints.

She nimbly ran through the combination and opened the safe. She had been careful to make sure that it was shut after the detective left that afternoon. "Yep, everything is still here."

"If there's nothing missing, we can write it up as vandalism or an attempted robbery. But it's not officially a burglary if nothing has been stolen."

Of course not.

"It'll take me a while to get everything back in order." Julie cringed at the thought. It was going to take hours.

"Take some pictures," Frost told the uniformed officer. "Then dust the safe." He pulled a small kit from his jacket pocket and handed it to the officer. Then he turned back to Julie. "Walk around; see if anything seems to be missing or out of place."

She looked pointedly at the mess that was once her neat and orderly office.

"You know what I mean," he said.

Julie studied the debris on the floor, trying to match it to her memory of the ledgers and books that had once been up on the shelves.

"Why did you call for an ambulance earlier?" Frost asked.

"One of the guests had a problem at dinner." It was the safest answer she could come up with.

"That's some problem if you needed an ambulance." Frost eyed her steadily.

"How did you know—?"

He shot her that patronizing smile again. "I make it my business to know. So, what happened?"

"We're still waiting on word from the hospital," Julie said. "But Joyce Fillmore had some sort of an attack while she was eating."

"One of the older ladies?" he asked.

"The tall one."

"Heart attack?"

"Maybe. Or a food allergy. Her friend said she was allergic to peanuts."

He took out his notebook and scribbled something on it. "Was your staff aware of this allergy?"

Julie crossed her arms and stared him down. "Of course we were." *Of course Hannah was.*

"Let me know what you find out." After the officer was finished taking pictures, Frost walked around the room looking for heaven only knew what. He used his pen to pull the curtain away from the window and peer out. Her office overlooked the back garden; though, whenever she was in the office, she didn't have much time for admiring the view. "When you first came in here, was there a window open?"

"No."

He let the curtain fall back into place. "Is it possible that the culprit came in through the hallway?"

She nodded. "Yes."

"Do you keep your office door locked?"

"Not ordinarily," she said. "Only when I'm leaving the inn."

"Did you leave the inn today?" he asked, still poking around the room, peering under things and behind things, never once looking at her while he spoke.

"No."

"So, it's feasible that any one of your guests or staff could have come in here and done this."

"Why do I feel like I'm the one being charged here?"

This time Frost looked at her, his smile genuinely apologetic. "It's been a long day, Miss Ellis."

"Tell me about it," she muttered.

"What was that?" he asked.

"I said, I'm sorry to hear that."

He smiled as if he knew that wasn't what she'd said at all. "We'll write up the report. In the meantime, you can feel free to clean this up."

She nodded.

"And one more thing, Miss Ellis."

Julie turned to face him.

"You should lock your office door whether you're here or not."

"Locking a door in Straussberg!" Shirley exclaimed. "Why, whoever heard of such a thing?"

"It seems to be my only recourse now," Julie said. Though, with the journal missing and her office a mess, it seemed a bit like closing the barn door after the horses had gotten out.

After leaving her office, Julie had walked to the tearoom to see if Shirley was still at the inn. She should have gone home long ago, but Julie was glad she'd remained for a while longer.

"I don't like it either," Julie added. She'd lived in places where people had to lock their doors at all times, but Straussberg had a different vibe. A small, country town feel. An everyone-knows-everyone kind of place. She hated the fact that it seemed to be changing right before her eyes.

"Of course, back in the day …," Shirley was saying.

Julie nodded politely. Time spent with Shirley was entertaining, to be sure, but she wouldn't classify it as relaxing. She tried her best to keep track of Shirley's colorful storytelling, but her mind kept wandering.

Perhaps whoever ransacked her office wasn't trying to find the journal. What if that person was merely trying to scare her? What if the art thieves who swore their revenge on her had finally caught up with her?

That made more sense than any of her other theories. Though the thought sent her heart sinking to her toes.

With as many tourists as had been in and out of the inn lately, it could have been anyone. Most had been gawkers, not registered guests. And there had been *a lot* of them. That narrowed the potential vandal down to … well, almost anyone in town.

Julie's phone buzzed in her pocket. "Excuse me," she said to Shirley, checking the screen before answering. She did not recognize the number.

"Julie dear, it's Sadie Davidson."

"Sadie! Good to hear from you. How is Joyce?"

"Well, they have her stabilized, but they're going to keep

her overnight to make sure she's OK. Personally, I think she's fine. She's sitting up in the bed, flirting shamelessly with the male nurses. I suspect she'll be right as rain by tomorrow."

Relief flooded through Julie. "I'm so glad to hear that. Have they determined what caused her collapse?"

"It was just as I suspected. Somehow she got ahold of some peanuts. We're lucky it didn't kill her right off."

ELEVEN

Julie had no more than hung up with Sadie and closed the door behind Shirley when she spotted Carrie meandering around near the tearoom.

"I thought you were going to bed," Julie said, bypassing a normal greeting.

Carrie jumped as if she hadn't been expecting Julie to say anything to her—or as if she hadn't noticed Julie at all. The petite girl bumped into the wall, nearly knocking a painting onto the floor.

"Sorry," she mumbled, pushing her glasses up on her nose and straightening the picture. It was more crooked when she was finished fixing it than it had been before she began.

"What are you doing down here?" Julie asked, her suspicions rising.

Carrie's eyes grew wide. "I thought I forgot something in the tearoom."

"Really? What was it? I'll help you look," Julie said with as much care and concern as she could muster.

"Uh, my handkerchief."

Julie blinked. Did anyone under the age of seventy carry a handkerchief anymore? "Unfortunately, it looks like Shirley has already closed up for the night. You'll have to ask her in the morning."

Carrie nodded and pushed at her sleeves. "OK. Good night then." She turned on her heel to leave.

"Is there something you'd like to tell me?" Julie asked.

Carrie paused for a moment and then slowly shook her

head. "No." Without another word she crept up the steps as quietly as she'd come.

Julie stood in the foyer and watched her leave, a jillion thoughts zinging through her head. Carrie seemed the least likely of the guests to commit a heinous crime. Julie doubted the petite blonde even had enough strength to wield the overlarge candlestick that had been used to knock Alice over the head. But her bizarre behavior ... always creeping around ... so jumpy when spoken to. ...

Was Carrie even in the room when Alice was murdered? Julie couldn't remember if Carrie had been there or not. The girl was just so quiet, as if she wanted everyone to forget she existed.

But had she been there?

Julie thought back to the minutes before the power went out and promptly blew out an irritated breath. That was the problem. She simply couldn't remember. Of course, at the time, she hadn't been concerned about *real* murders. She hadn't been watching everyone with suspicious eyes. Her attention had been focused on making sure the murder part of the mystery went off without a hitch and on gearing up for a weekend of solving a fake murder ... not a *real* murder.

Julie rolled her shoulders, trying to ease some of the kinks out of her neck and back. On a whim, she started toward the back of the inn, where Hannah's room was located. The power had gone off right before the dessert service. *Had Carrie been in the room at the time?*

She lightly rapped on Hannah's door.

"It's open," came the soft reply.

Julie opened the door and found Hannah propped up on the bed as if she'd been expecting her friend to drop by.

"You're up late," Julie said.

Hannah shrugged. "Too much excitement, I guess, but I need to turn in soon. Morning comes quickly around here. Did you hear from Sadie?"

Julie nodded. "It was peanuts, but Joyce is going to be fine."

Hannah's eyes widened. "I'll clean out the pantry tomorrow. I don't know how it happened—maybe some type of cross-contamination."

Or purposeful contamination, Julie thought. "I'm sure it was just an unfortunate accident."

"Still." Hannah was clearly distraught over the incident.

Julie suspected Hannah would throw out the remaining ingredients from the evening meal and offer to pay for it herself if need be.

"I need you to think back for a moment," Julie said. "Do you remember seeing Carrie at the dining table Friday night?"

"Of course."

"OK. But was she there when you served the entrée?"

"Yes. Well, I'm pretty sure." Hannah frowned as she tried to recall. "I mean, I took her a plate. She had to have been there. You don't think—?"

"I don't know." Julie perched on the edge of Hannah's small bed. "The problem is, I can't remember that specific detail."

"Even if she wasn't at the table, that doesn't mean she killed Alice." Hannah sat up a little taller. "Also, if she hadn't been there, don't you think someone would have mentioned it?"

"You're right." Julie ran her hand through her hair, an unthinking gesture she often did when she was frustrated.

"Although, she does have an amazing ability to go unnoticed," Hannah said.

Julie was going to be so glad when this weekend was over. In less than twenty-four hours, crime solved or not, the police had to at least let the guests leave town. That time couldn't come soon enough.

Julie pushed up from the bed and smiled at her friend. "Get some sleep. I'll see you at breakfast."

Hannah murmured her goodnight as Julie let herself out of the room.

She heard the lock click into place as she started down the hall.

Julie made her way through the kitchen, resisting the urge to grab a snack. True, dinner had been a complete fiasco. She'd eaten only about half of her meal before Joyce collapsed. And after that, her appetite had done a swift disappearing act—until now. But hungry or not, eating this late was not good for the thighs, no matter how tasty that last piece of cinnamon cake looked.

She walked toward the front of the inn for one last check before she headed upstairs.

"Can I talk to you for a minute?"

"Gah!" Julie whirled around, hand pressed to her chest. "Carrie!" she gasped. "I thought you went to bed."

Carrie shook her head and stared at the scuffed toes of her ugly brown shoes. "I just needed some time to …" She glanced off to the side, seeming to look at nothing as she bit her lip. "I need to tell you something."

Julie could hardly miss the ominous tone in Carrie's words. "All right. What is it?"

"Can we talk somewhere private?"

"How about we take a walk?" Julie suggested. She couldn't bear the thought of sitting across from Carrie and watching her shrink under her gaze.

Carrie nodded, and the two of them made their way to the back door in silence.

The night breeze had turned cool, and Carrie pulled her too-big sweater a little tighter around her. Julie wished she'd taken the time to put on something with sleeves. Instead, she rubbed the goose bumps on her arms and led the way to the garden path.

The air was filled with the perfume of sweet violets and hyacinths. Julie inhaled the soothing scents and waited for Carrie to begin, bracing herself for whatever was to come.

Finally, the girl drew in a deep breath and said, "I know where the book is."

Julie stopped dead in her tracks.

Carrie continued to walk on, stumbling a bit as the path grew uneven. She paused when she realized she'd left Julie behind.

Julie forced her feet into motion. "You mean the Civil War journal?"

Carrie nodded.

"You know where it is—right this very moment?"

"Well, I know where it *was*."

"OK ... that's good news. I think." Julie motioned to a small wooden bench. "Why don't you start at the beginning?"

Carrie took a seat and seemed to mull over her words as if deciding on the best place to start. "Fr-Friday night at dinner, I had to go to the bathroom."

"Was this before or after Alice—?"

"Before." Carrie ducked her head and twisted her hands in her lap. "I had just finished my entrée, and I thought I should go before we started dessert. I was pretty sure I could get to the bathroom and back before the 'big moment' in the mystery play."

The big moment that never happened.

"So, I slipped out and went to the restroom that's down

the hall from your office. I was washing my hands when the power went off." She gave a delicate shudder. "It was unnerving to be in such a closed space with it so dark, so I dried my hands as quickly as possible and stepped out into the hall. I figured the mystery had begun, and I wanted to get back to my seat before the lights came back on. Unfortunately, the hallway was as dark as the bathroom."

Julie nodded encouragingly, though inside she was praying that Carrie didn't confess to the murder right there on the garden bench.

"So, I'm standing there in the hall," Carrie said, "and I see someone coming toward me." She paused, furrowing her brows. "He held a flashlight in one hand and the book in the other."

"He?" Julie asked. "You're saying it was a man?"

"I think so." She wrinkled her nose in uncertainty. "The light flashed in my eyes, and it was hard to see."

Of course. Julie tried not to let her frustration show. But she suspected whoever Carrie saw holding the light and the book was also responsible for the power outage. How else would they have known that a flashlight would be needed?

"All right. So you *think* it was a man," Julie said. "What about the book?"

"It was definitely the journal you showed us."

"Are you absolutely sure?" Julie asked. "It was dark. You're not even certain if a man or woman was holding it."

"I'm sure." Carrie untwisted her fingers, seeming to grow a little more relaxed as she continued her story. "I think I surprised him as much as he surprised me. But I knew he wasn't supposed to have the book."

"Even though you couldn't see his face?"

"It wasn't his book," Carrie said.

"True enough."

"But when I said as much, he jeered at me."

Jeered? Julie frowned.

"So I took it from him. The lights came back on, and he ran away before I could get a good look at him. I put the book in the game cabinet and went back into the dining room."

"Why did you hide the book in the game cabinet?"

Carrie began to fidget again. "I don't know. I figured the evening was about to start. I could always go back and get it later and return it to you then."

Julie shook her head. "OK. You went back into the dining room. What happened next?"

"That was when Susan started screaming," Carrie said.

"So, the journal is in the game cabinet?" It took every ounce of Julie's willpower not to spring off the bench and go look.

Carrie shook her head sadly. "I went back for it the next morning, but it was gone."

Deflated, Julie slumped back on the bench. "Why did you wait so long to go back for it?"

"It was late by the time the police left." Carrie shrugged. "I've been … working a lot lately and needed some rest. I figured it was safe enough, hidden in the cabinet, so I went on to bed."

Julie didn't miss the small pause before the word "working." She asked, "What kind of work do you do?"

"This and that." Carrie jumped to her feet like Jack springing from his box. "I guess I should go to bed now. That's all I wanted to tell you. Good night." She started to leave, but Julie stopped her.

"Why didn't you tell me this before now?" Julie asked, struggling to keep her anger at bay.

"I wasn't sure how you would take it."

"And you have absolutely no guess as to who the mystery person in the hallway might have been? Not even an inkling?"

Carrie shook her head, but Julie got the impression the girl was still holding something back.

"I'm glad you told me," Julie said, giving Carrie a reassuring smile. "Do you think the thief saw you put the journal in the game cabinet?"

"No." Carrie pushed at her sleeves again. "I was all alone when I stashed it."

Julie sighed with defeat. *Given the number of visitors we've had meandering through the inn this weekend, anyone could have the journal now.*

After Carrie went upstairs for the third time that evening, Julie promptly checked the game cabinet.

The old cabinet sat outside the dining room near the first-floor sitting room. Board games, decks of cards, dominos, and more were stacked inside. The purpose of the cabinet was to encourage guests to enjoy one another's company and also add to the homey atmosphere that Millie had created. After all, man could not live by quilting alone.

But Julie hadn't seen too many guests play with the games during their stay. Most times, they preferred to be out touring the town, quilting, or visiting with resident storyteller Shirley.

As quietly as she could, Julie removed all the games from the cabinet and set them neatly to the side, perusing through boxes as she went, to see if by some strange deed, the journal had ended up inside one of them. But the effort proved useless. The book simply wasn't there.

With a sigh, she began the arduous task of putting everything back inside, fitting the boxes together in the small space like a jigsaw puzzle. The fact was, any tourist or guest with a dishonest bent could have happened by during all the commotion over the last three days and taken the book. The list of possible thieves was a mile long.

If the culprit was one of the visitors, then there wasn't a single thing she could do.

But if it was one of the guests ...

Julie stood and started climbing the stairs toward her room on the third floor. She found the second floor quiet except for the gentle snores of one of her guests. If she had to guess, she'd say Kenneth. He looked like a snorer.

The third floor was even quieter. She wasn't sure if it was because Carrie had gone to sleep already or because she was just being her normal wallflower self.

Once inside her room, Julie rolled the tension from her neck and changed into her pajamas. It seemed like a lifetime ago since she'd dressed for the day. So much had happened since the morning.

She padded to the bathroom, pulled her thick hair back into a sloppy ponytail, and washed her face. Once her teeth were brushed, she turned out the light and crawled beneath the covers. Her body was more than ready to give in to the urge to get some much-needed rest.

But her mind was not. She squeezed her eyes shut as her thoughts raced.

Should she call Detective Frost and tell him what Carrie had relayed to her? She figured she should, but the last thing she wanted to do was face the detective's keen eyes again so soon. There were times when his attitude made her feel like he believed she brought all of this onto herself, as if Straussberg had never experienced any real crime until she showed up.

No, she wouldn't call him. At least not right now. She was bone weary and not in the mood. If she was going to call anyone at this hour, it would be Daniel Franklin. She could use a dose of his deep voice and charming smile. Maybe she would call him tomorrow. Or if luck was truly on her side, he would drop in to see how things were going.

As if that's going to happen. She hadn't had much in the way of good luck since she'd set foot on Missouri soil.

Twelve

"Julie," a male voice said.

She turned to see Liam rushing down the stairs toward her the next morning.

He smiled politely. "Can I talk to you for a moment?"

"Of course," she said, though what she really wanted to do was duck into the tearoom and snatch another cup of coffee. Coming off of a fitful night of very little sleep, she knew she'd need all of the caffeine she could get to survive the day.

"I know I'm supposed to leave tonight, but I was wondering if I could rent my room for a while longer."

Julie blinked. "You want to stay here *longer*?"

"Yes." He nodded eagerly.

"For how many more days?"

He shrugged and didn't meet her eyes. "I'm not sure."

"I take it you've found the weekend to be inspiring fodder for your next book."

He had the good graces to blush. "When did you figure it out?"

"Friday."

He rubbed a palm against the back of his neck. "Thanks for not telling everyone my secret. Sometimes I just need time to be plain old me."

"I understand, and you're welcome," she said. "But don't thank me too much. Sadie figured it out as well."

"Huh. So, about the room …?" he asked.

"I'm sure we can work something out. I do have rooms available."

"That's precisely what I was hoping you'd say." With a satisfied grin, he started back up the staircase, taking them two at a time.

"Aren't you coming to breakfast?" Julie called to him.

"I've got something to do. Then I'll be down," he called over his shoulder.

Gregory, Carrie, Susan, Kenneth, and Sadie were already in the breakfast room when Julie arrived.

Julie was glad to see Sadie looking none the worse for wear. "When did you get back?"

"Late last night." Sadie took a delicate sip of her tea.

"Did Joyce come with you?" Julie asked.

"Oh no, dear, she's still at the hospital. Poor thing. The doctor made her stay a little while longer." The older woman shifted in her seat and took another sip. "I couldn't stand it there for another minute. Hospital food and all that. Dreadful smells, you know."

"Oh." Julie wasn't sure how to respond. The two women had been inseparable since they had arrived, the best of friends—or so she'd thought. Julie had fully expected Sadie to remain with Joyce until she was released from the hospital, not be chased away by a little thing like smelly hospital food. Did Sadie have an ulterior motive for returning to the inn so soon?

"I hope they release her today," Julie finally said.

"Thank you, dear. So do I."

Julie turned her focus to the rest of the group just in time to hear Kenneth exclaim, "I'm just saying that I don't believe we have anything else to worry about!"

"I don't see how you can possibly believe that." Susan frowned.

"It's simple, really." Kenneth picked up a scone and

slathered it with clotted cream. Julie could almost see Hannah roll her eyes. With all the work Hannah put into her fabulous scones, they didn't need any embellishment, not even the traditional topping the Brits used. "It's the law of averages. So much has already happened, what more could feasibly go wrong?"

Susan shook her head. "You shouldn't have uttered that challenge to the universe."

"All I know is I'll be glad to get out of here," Gregory chimed in with his usual scowl firmly in place.

Julie noticed he'd brought the small bronze duck from his room and set it next to his plate. Not quite as menacing a weapon as the fire poker, but potentially lethal all the same. She grabbed a cup of coffee and sat down next to Shirley.

"Good morning," the spunky redhead greeted as Julie joined her. As was the case on most days, her attitude was just as lively as her clothing—a bright pink-and-red dress accented with dangly heart earrings and a handwoven scarf.

Julie thought she looked like a walking valentine, but Shirley always brought a smile to her lips. "Good morning to you."

"It's going to rain today," Shirley announced loudly enough so everyone would hear.

"It's already started." Julie stirred a bit of cream and sugar into her coffee and took a tentative sip. *Perfect.*

"Great." Gregory tossed his napkin onto his plate and snorted in disgust. "Our last day here, and we're trapped inside this place."

"I'd be happy to loan you an umbrella," Julie offered.

Gregory simply rolled his eyes.

"A pity. I was looking forward to one last day in town," Sadie agreed.

"It should stop later this afternoon," Shirley said.

"I think it's a perfect time to work on the quilt. We're almost done," Julie reminded them.

"Yeah, like *that's* what I want to do," Gregory said sarcastically. He propped his feet in the chair opposite him as if daring someone to tell him to get them down.

"We could play board games," Kenneth suggested.

"What did I miss?" Liam sauntered into the breakfast room.

"Nothing except that it's going to rain," Shirley said.

"It already is." Liam snatched a piece of fruit and a couple of muffins from the sideboard and then poured himself a cup of coffee.

"We were right in the middle of deciding what to do today," Susan said.

"Quilting or board games," Carrie added. "What's your choice?"

"Quilt," Sadie said.

Liam shook his head. "I have some stuff to work on in my room."

A chorus of protests went up around the room. Julie couldn't decide if they honestly wanted Liam's company or if they wanted to keep an eye on him.

"If I have to stay down here and endure this, so do you," Gregory said. "And I vote for playing a game."

Julie could see Liam begin to cave. "Come on," she said. "It'll be fun."

Liam looked like he might protest further, but then he seemed to change his mind. "All right. Count me in."

"Yay," Carrie said. "What do you want to play?"

"Anything but Clue," Gregory grumped.

Julie couldn't help but chuckle at the absurdity of his comment and the situation as a whole.

After everyone finished breakfast, most of the group moved to the tearoom where the quilt was set up, while Kenneth and Liam went to get the games out of the game cabinet.

"How about Othello?" Liam asked.

"But that's a two-person game," Susan protested.

"Fine by me," Gregory said. "You and somebody else can play and leave the rest of us in peace."

"Well, there's Monopoly, Life, and Trivial Pursuit."

"I am not playing a trivia game with a college professor," Kenneth said. "All the brown questions will be too easy for you."

"Like you'd be any better," Liam protested. "You're a doctor. You'd get all the science ones right."

Kenneth smiled. "Touché."

"Maybe we should play teams," Susan suggested.

"Or we could have a checkers tournament," Julie said. "Whoever isn't playing can quilt. How does that sound?"

"I like it," Carrie said.

They drew numbers to see who would go first. Gregory and Kenneth drew one and two, and had first play. Carrie, Sadie, and Susan looked somewhat relieved to be quilting while the men moved their red and black discs across the board.

Liam slid into the seat next to Julie. "Say, you wouldn't happen to have any rooms available on the first floor, would you?"

"Sorry, no," Julie said. "The guest rooms are all located on the second floor, except for the Tower Room, where Carrie is staying."

"Too bad."

The inn manager inside Julie kicked in. "Is there something wrong with your room?"

"My room is fine," Liam said. "But I thought it might be more fun to be down here."

"I would have thought you'd need quiet and solitude."

Liam shook his head. "I like to be in the thick of things. I find it inspiring."

"For your writing," Carrie interjected.

Liam swung around to stare at her. "How did you know?"

The young woman smiled. "Your picture is on your jacket covers."

Liam seemed to puff up with pride. "And you've read my books?"

"Every one of them."

"Me too," Susan said.

"And me too, dear," Sadie said.

He looked back to Julie. "Does everyone here know who I am?"

She shrugged. "Don't look at me. I didn't tell them."

He turned to Carrie. "Why didn't you say something?"

"I figured that if you wanted to hide out badly enough that you lied about your name, you needed some time to be someone else."

Liam's expression softened. "Thank you very much for that."

"Well, unless we're going to host an impromptu book signing and group therapy session, can we get back to the game?" Gregory asked.

Kenneth turned his attention back to the board.

"If you want to change rooms simply for a change of scenery," Julie said to Liam, "you could have the Tower Room once it's free. You'd have a completely different view—though it's certainly not in the thick of things."

"Thanks. I will."

"Is something wrong with your room?" Kenneth asked.

Gregory sighed and leaned back in his seat, clearly more than ready to get the game over with.

"Nah," Liam said. "I was just hoping to get on the first floor."

"Our room's got that great view over the garden," Kenneth said. "That might be inspiring."

"You're not leaving today?" Carrie asked Liam.

"Nope. I've rented my room for a little while longer."

She nodded and went back to her quilting.

"You know, that's a brilliant idea." Kenneth's entire face lit up. "Let's stay a while longer, hon."

Susan looked like she was about to choke, but she managed to keep it together. "Shouldn't we get back to your practice? I mean, we've been away longer than we'd anticipated."

"Just a day." Kenneth looked back to the board and made a triple jump. "King me," he said to Gregory. "This is the most fun I've had in years."

Stunned at the strange turn of events, Julie nodded. "It might take a bit of shuffling, but I do have one more room open for the rest of the week."

"And we can keep our same room?"

"Unless you still want to trade with Liam."

"Liam's room's bigger," Shirley chimed in.

"Then let's do it," Kenneth said. "What do you say, Liam?"

The two men smiled like they had pulled off the biggest heist in history. They stood and started talking about how to best go about switching out.

"I'll get Inga to change the sheets," Shirley said.

Susan pushed back from the quilt, muttering something about terrible vacations.

"Hey, what about our game?" Gregory hollered as Liam and Kenneth left the tearoom to go upstairs. They either didn't hear him or they ignored him. Julie wasn't sure which.

Carrie continued to quilt, seemingly satisfied with her morning plans.

Julie stood and went to make the changes to the register. There for a moment, even with Gregory in the room, the vibe had seemed almost … normal. Her guests were playing checkers, quilting, drinking tea, and otherwise having a fairly good time—all things considered.

How long can it possibly last?

Carrie and Sadie continued to quilt as Liam and the Calhouns switched rooms. It took the better part of the morning, but at least they were all occupied.

Julie made her way to the kitchen around ten.

As usual, Hannah was mixing up something that smelled yeasty and delicious.

"I was wondering if we could serve something for lunch today," Julie asked.

Hannah frowned. "I wasn't planning on it."

"I know, but it's raining, and everyone seems to be content to stay here. Most of the guests wouldn't normally be here right now." Had it not been for the murder, everyone already would have been checked out and on their way home.

Hannah gave Julie that look, the one that said she was overstepping her boundaries.

"It doesn't have to be anything elaborate," Julie said. "Maybe some finger foods and snacks. That way they can continue to quilt and play games. No one has to stop if they don't want to."

Hannah grumbled in response.

"So, you'll whip something up?"

"Of course."

Julie smiled. "Thanks. I'll let everyone know."

It was almost noon before Kenneth, Susan, and Liam came back downstairs.

"How did a single guy get such a big room?" Kenneth asked.

"Oh, it's not that big," Liam said, with a shrug.

"I can't believe you're giving that up."

"All in the name of art," Liam said. "And the view of the garden."

Kenneth beamed at his new friend.

Julie suspected he either wanted a book signed or the next story dedicated to him.

Carrie sat up straight when they entered the tearoom. She stretched the kinks out of her back and adjusted her glasses. "Susan, will you quilt with me?"

Susan smiled. "Of course."

"It's our turn at checkers," Kenneth said, clapping Liam on the back.

They sat at the table where the board was set up. Kenneth and Gregory's abandoned game was still in place. The men started realigning the pieces as Hannah entered carrying a tray of tiny quiches and finger sandwiches.

"Thank you," Julie said as Hannah set the tray on a nearby table. "Normally we don't serve lunch, but Hannah didn't want you to have to go out in the rain, especially since she's the best chef in town."

Murmured thanks went up all around. Hannah blushed, privately rolling her eyes at Julie.

"I'll leave it up here buffet style," Hannah said. "You can help yourselves when you're ready."

"It looks wonderful," Julie said, convinced the woman was a miracle worker.

Hannah shot her a look that would have meant "You owe me one," but the sparkle in her eyes said otherwise. Julie knew her friend really was happy cooking for the inn's guests. After all the excitement they'd shared over the years, it was amazing that the simple act of cooking could bring Hannah such joy.

Julie took a bite of one of the quiches. *OK. Maybe not so simple.* It was fabulous. She managed to swallow her satisfied moan with the bite and not embarrass herself in front of her guests.

Kenneth and Liam grabbed plates and filled them as high as they would go.

Shirley made fresh coffee and a pot of tea.

Carrie and Susan continued to quilt, unwilling to stop and eat, and also respectful enough of the hard work they'd put in to not risk staining the beautiful creation before they even finished it.

As Julie picked up one more quiche, it suddenly dawned on her that something was wrong with the scene before her. Somebody was missing. "Where's Gregory?"

"I saw him headed toward the library a little bit ago," Shirley said. "He's still gone?"

Julie scanned the faces before her as if she could possibly miss him in a crowd of six. "Yes."

"Oh, well I'm sure he'll be right back," Shirley said.

Julie had a bad feeling about it. She muttered a response and headed out of the tearoom, intent on finding Gregory. But the library was empty.

She slowly made her way back toward the others, poking her head into various rooms as she went. It wasn't like he couldn't leave the inn, but she was suspicious all the same. As she passed the door to the tearoom on the way to check the library, she heard Shirley say in her most dramatic voice, "… and would you like to know how this mystery ends?"

Boy, would I, she thought with a grim smile.

THIRTEEN

Realizing Shirley was talking about the murder mystery weekend, Julie changed course and headed back into the tearoom.

"Yes, yes, tell us please," Susan and Carrie said over each other.

The men smiled indulgently at them.

"Well," Shirley drawled in that way she had that pulled everyone to the edge of their seats before she even got to the good stuff. Her flair for the dramatic had made her twice-weekly sessions of Stitches and Stories one of the inn's most popular events with guests and tourists alike. "My character's name was Shelly Carson, and I was married to Bill Carson. That was Daniel Franklin from the other night. Remember him?"

Everyone nodded.

"But I'd been having an affair with Brandon Waters. He was the young man who came on Friday as well." She waggled her eyebrows in a "hubba-hubba" sort of way.

"Are you going to tell them the entire plot?" Julie asked.

"What choice do I have? Half a plot won't make a very good story." Shirley smiled. "Don't worry. I'll write another one for next year."

Julie nearly choked. *Like there's going to be another one next year.*

"Unbeknownst to me, my husband, Bill, found out about my affair with Brandon. A jealous man, he planned on killing Brandon with poisoned wine. Instead, Inga accidentally drinks the wine, falls to the floor dead, and begins the murder mystery weekend."

"That's it?" Kenneth asked.

"It was to be much more involved than that. You would go searching for clues. There was a picture of me with Brandon and a couple of other things for you to find … a bottle marked 'poison' that was really water with a little bit of almond extract in it. That sort of thing."

Liam stroked his chin. Julie could almost see the wheels turning in his mind. She wondered if Shirley's story would end up as plot points in his own.

"Carrie, come play checkers with me," Kenneth said. "Liam's lost in his own world."

Carrie shook her head. "No thanks. I'd rather quilt."

Liam stood. "If you don't mind, I think I'll go lie down for a while."

Julie felt certain that was code for "write another chapter." But she wasn't concerned. Not anymore. Even though the murder still hadn't been solved, her part as hostess for the weekend was quickly drawing to a close—and not soon enough for her.

"Susan, honey."

Susan looked up to find her husband nodding at her.

"Play checkers with me?" he asked.

She rose from her seat and went to the table where he sat, never once taking her eyes from him.

With everyone settled once more, Julie decided to continue her search for Gregory, only then realizing that Sadie had disappeared as well. "Where's Sadie?"

Carrie looked up from her quilting and pushed her glasses back into place. "She was here a little while ago."

"Maybe she went to her room to lie down," Susan said.

"Perhaps," Julie murmured in return. It was a feasible conclusion, considering the night she'd had with her friend.

Julie climbed the stairs to find Inga stripping beds and piling sheets in the hallway.

"Is Sadie up here?" Julie asked.

Inga shook her head.

"Gregory?"

"Just me."

"Hmm." Julie headed back the way she'd come. After a thorough search of the downstairs failed to turn up either of the missing guests, she decided they must have left the inn.

She popped her head into the kitchen, where Hannah was at work as hard as ever.

"How was lunch?" Hannah asked.

"Delicious. You outdid yourself."

Hannah smiled in a way that said she had known that all along.

Julie stepped inside and slid onto one of the stools at the center island. She picked up a bottle of herbs sitting near Hannah's latest project and sniffed appreciatively. "Mmm ... rosemary."

"So what now?" Hannah asked. "We just wait to see if the detective gets this mess wrapped up before nine o'clock tonight?"

"Unfortunately, I'm not sure what else we can do. And with the exception of Gregory, everyone seems to be getting along well enough. I don't anticipate any more verbal battles to break out between now and when they'll be free to leave town."

"So, all's quiet in Straussberg?"

Julie snorted. "*Quiet* might be a stretch. We both know something sinister is lurking beneath this peaceful façade."

Hannah nodded. "Any more leads on the journal?"

"No." Julie slid off her stool. "And on that note, I'm going to the basement to see if I can find anything else to donate for the auction."

"You really don't think the book will turn up?"

Julie shook her head.

"Are you convinced someone stole it?"

"I don't know what I think," Julie said. "But I need something to put in the auction."

"Happy hunting."

Julie gave her friend a small salute before grabbing the large key ring off the hook on the wall, flipping the light switch at the top of the stairs, and heading toward the cellar.

The bulbs were dim, caked with dust from years past.

Other than her initial trip into the cellar with Daniel and her quest to find something of value hidden in the old wooden crates Millie had stacked in one corner, Julie normally avoided the cellar. She kept the door locked at all times as it was a potential hazard. The condition of the room hadn't changed much in the couple of weeks since she'd last ventured into the dusty, dank space beneath the inn. A thick layer of grime still coated everything that she hadn't touched during her previous visits, and the places where she had been were already covered in a light layer of new dust.

She eased down the final rickety step of the staircase. She wasn't afraid of the cellar itself; she was fearful of what was above it. The whole space seemed shaky, like one slight tremble of the earth could bring everything tumbling down on top of her.

Ridiculous. Quit fretting and find something to donate.

The inn was as sound as a pound, as Millie would say. Not to mention that two walls of the cellar were cut out of sheer rock.

Julie picked her way to the crates where she'd found the journal. She hadn't seen much else in there the last time, but she'd been very focused on the journal. When she found it, she quit looking and raced up the stairs to check it out.

Only when she got it upstairs did she discover that it wasn't a journal but a manual with writing in the margins.

She'd heard about such things. There wasn't a lot to do in 1861 with war all around. Most of the military volunteers had been given blank journals to help them fill any downtime. Most wrote letters back home. Those men who hadn't been issued journals used what they had on them—from favorite books to government-issued publications given to them by their commanders.

Julie opened the crate full of old books and picked through them. The ones on the top she'd already seen—old copies of books that might be worth something to the right bidder, though she doubted there were any bibliophiles in Straussberg, Missouri. She stacked them to the side on top of one of the other crates that contained empty canning jars. She made a mental note to ask Millie if she could see if the local library had any interest in them.

Toward the bottom she found a couple more books—a hardcover copy of *To Kill a Mockingbird* that could possibly be a first edition and a leather-bound edition of *The Adventures of Huckleberry Finn.*

She checked both for a signature. Neither had one, but they could still be valuable. She dusted them off and then brushed her hands together. Like *that* did any good.

Julie stacked the books one on top of the other and started back up the steps.

It wasn't easy juggling two dusty books while trying to remain clean and relock the door to the basement, but somehow she managed.

She carted the books into her office, completely forgetting the mess that awaited her. But when she set foot inside, everything appeared to be in perfect order.

"Inga strikes again," she mused, grateful for the woman's superhero-like efficiency.

Carefully, Julie placed the books on the desk. Then she hustled down the hall to wash her hands. She was amazed at how quiet it was in the inn today. She smiled a little to herself. *May it last.*

But it didn't.

The sound of a startled shout stopped her in her tracks. She quickly tried to determine if the noise was coming from outside or upstairs. There was another louder shout and then a sickening thud, like a body hitting the floor.

Julie raced down the hall, nearly colliding with Shirley as she rounded the corner from the tearoom with Carrie hot on her heels. Hannah burst through the kitchen door.

"I thought I heard screams. What happened?" Hannah demanded.

"I'm not sure." Julie quickly led the small group upstairs, checking first in Kenneth and Susan's room, and then hurrying down the hall to Liam's new room.

Shock was too mild a word for what she saw when she opened the door. "Liam!" she exclaimed.

Liam Preston looked up from where he stood, looming over the body of Kenneth sprawled on the floor, a lamp in his hand.

Fourteen

As soon as he caught sight of his audience, Liam dropped the lamp. It bounced off Kenneth's legs before hitting the floor.

Liam ran shaking fingers through his hair. "I-I didn't mean to …" His voice quavered. "I didn't mean to kill him!"

Carrie gasped and turned her head away.

Liam collapsed onto the edge of the bed and covered his face with his hands. Julie knelt by Kenneth, feeling for a pulse.

"What's going on in here?" Susan demanded from the doorway, struggling to see past the bodies in front of her. She let out a strangled scream when she caught sight of her husband lying on the ground.

"Oh, Kenneth! Is he …?" Susan couldn't finish.

"He's alive," Julie said pushing back to her feet.

She made the announcement just as Inga joined the fray. The housekeeper took one look at the bloodied rug around Kenneth and shook her head, muttering something in German.

"Hannah—" Julie began.

"I'm on it." Hannah turned and marched out of the room with Inga close behind.

Susan knelt by her husband, gingerly touching his face. "Kenneth, can you hear me?"

Judging by the weird look on Susan's face, Julie had a feeling the woman was in shock.

"How long do you think he'll be out?" Shirley whispered.

"I have no idea," Julie answered.

"Are you sure he's not …" Liam swallowed hard.

"Unless dead people have pulses, I'm sure."

Susan brushed Kenneth's hair back from his face and continued to talk to him.

In record time, Inga and Hannah returned. They carried smelling salts, a bottle of peroxide, a couple of towels, and a bag of frozen peas between them.

"Here." Hannah handed the smelling salts to Julie. "I found these in the first-aid kit."

Julie snapped open the packet and held it under Kenneth's nose.

He stirred, swatting away the offensive odor as he struggled to sit up.

"Oh, thank heavens!" Susan exclaimed. She threw her arms around him, further hampering his progress.

Untangling himself from Susan's arms, Kenneth tried to get on his feet, but he failed miserably. "What happened?" He winced as he spoke, squinting as though trying to focus.

"I am so sorry," Liam said. "I thought you were the killer. What were you doing, sneaking around in my room?"

Kenneth gingerly touched his head, drawing his hand away to look at the blood on his fingers. "You *hit* me?"

"I'm sure it was just a simple misunderstanding," Julie said. "Wasn't it, Liam?" *Please say it was.*

Susan's eyes reflected the plea.

"What were you doing in my room?" Liam demanded again.

Kenneth sighed. "Can someone help me up?"

"Oh, right." Liam and Julie managed to hoist Kenneth onto his unsteady feet and over to the Queen Anne chair in the corner.

Hannah handed him the bag of peas covered with one of the towels. He winced as he held it in place on his head. Susan knelt at his feet, clasping his free hand in both of hers.

Inga brushed past all of them to work on the carpet.

"I suppose I have a confession to make," Kenneth began. "I couldn't sleep Saturday night. So I rummaged around in the game cabinet. I thought maybe I could get a deck of cards and play solitaire or something."

"The cabinet downstairs?" Julie asked.

Kenneth's nod turned into a wince. "Yes."

Everyone waited for him to continue.

"I found the journal in the cabinet. You know, the one you showed us Friday afternoon? I couldn't imagine how it got there, and I knew everyone was running around trying to find it." He grinned sheepishly. "So I hid it."

"You *what*?" Julie said. She'd practically turned the house upside down trying to find the stupid book. And all the time, Kenneth knew where it was? "Why didn't you say something?"

He shrugged. "Things were just getting exciting around here, and I was really starting to enjoy myself."

"You're saying you did this to try and keep up the level of excitement?" Julie asked, incredulous. As if murder wasn't excitement enough.

"It sounds dumb when *you* say it."

"It would sound dumb when *anyone* said it," Inga interjected from where she knelt on the floor, cleaning.

Kenneth frowned at her. "Plus, I didn't think anyone would believe that I just *found* it. I didn't want you all to think I was a thief."

No one spoke.

"So … I decided to hide it and see what happened," Kenneth continued. "When we switched rooms with Liam, I forgot all about where I hid it until this afternoon. I waited until he was asleep and tried to sneak in here and get it. The next thing I knew, you were waving ammonia under my nose."

"I truly am sorry," Liam said. "I was sound asleep. I didn't get a lot of rest last night. Then I heard something in my room. I didn't look. I just reacted. After what happened to Alice—"

"It's OK." Kenneth smiled as if to say "No hard feelings."

"Where is the book now?" Julie demanded.

Kenneth pushed himself to his feet and wobbled over to the closet. He tried to reach up for something on the shelf, but looked like he might swoon. He turned back to Liam. "Can you?"

Liam nodded and took his place in front of the closet, running his hands along the top shelf until he found what he was looking for. He pulled down the small leather book and offered it to Julie as if it were the crown jewels on a velvet pillow.

"For the last time, I do not want to go to the doctor," Kenneth said.

Liam and Inga had managed to get him downstairs and seated in the tearoom. He looked like he'd rather sleep, but they were afraid he might have a concussion.

Once Susan learned that her husband was going to be all right, she declared she had a migraine and went to her room. Carrie, who had been comforting Susan, claimed she wanted to work on the quilt. "Sewing always calms my nerves," she stated. Too bad the same thing didn't work for Susan.

"Move the peas," Julie told Kenneth.

He did as she ordered, and she made a face as she examined the cut. It was large enough and deep enough to need stitches, but the stubborn man would have nothing to do with it. Not to mention the inevitable concussion. "It needs sutures," she said for the umpteenth time.

"I'm fine. Doctors are overpriced. I should know; I am one."

"The inn will gladly pay for the visit." It was one thing to have to pay for an ER visit and quite another to foot the bill for an ICU stay after he slipped into a coma.

She reached toward him as if to help him to his feet.

He smacked her hand away. "I'm fine, I tell you."

"Stitches," she said again, already tired of this game.

"Superglue," he countered. "I'll glue it shut, and it'll be healed in no time."

It was better than nothing. "How are you going to do it? It's on the back of your head."

"You'll help me?" It was almost a question.

"No. But I'll drive you to the doctor."

As if by magic, Inga appeared, carrying the tiny tube of glue. She had rubber gloves on her hands and a determined look on her face. "I'll take care of it. Move."

For a brief moment, Kenneth looked like he might change his mind. But instead he nodded and turned so that Inga could get to the wound.

"Ow, ow, ow," he protested as she held the sides in place and squeezed glue onto the area.

"Hold still." Her German accent seemed more pronounced than usual, as if she was trying to scare Kenneth. It worked. Once finished, a ghost of a smile played at the corners of her lips as she pulled off the gloves and marched out of the room.

Julie stepped behind Kenneth and inspected the repair.

"How's it look?" he asked.

"Better," she said. At least the glue had sealed the area enough that it wasn't bleeding any longer. No doubt that was Inga's primary motivation—to keep any more blood from staining the floors.

Liam stepped forward. "I truly am sorry."

"If you apologize to me again, I'm going to take the nearest lamp and knock you in the head with it," Kenneth said.

Julie sincerely hoped not. But she hid her smile as the two sat down to the checkerboard. With the conk on the head Kenneth had received, she had a feeling Liam was about to win all the afternoon games.

She stopped in her office long enough to deposit the journal in the safe, giving the dial an extra spin to ensure it locked properly, and then made her way to the kitchen.

There was still no sign of Gregory or Sadie anywhere. It seemed strange that they would both disappear so quickly and simultaneously. Still, she reminded herself that they were under no obligation to let her know what they were up to. They could do as they liked, as long as it was in town.

Hannah was in the kitchen, sitting at the island with a cup of coffee at her elbow and a large cookbook propped open in front of her.

"Time for a little reading?" Julie asked.

"Just trying to keep the menu fresh. This weekend has seriously challenged my repertoire."

Julie crossed the room and poured herself a cup of coffee. She added cream and a bit of sugar, and then joined her friend at the island. "You know I think you do a wonderful job, right?"

Hannah smiled. "I know, but it never hurts to keep on one's toes."

Now that was a philosophy that Julie could embrace.

"Thanks for all your help this morning," Julie said. "This weekend, actually."

Hannah shrugged. "What are friends for?"

The phone rang. Julie crossed to the old-fashioned unit hanging on the wall. The crazy thing even had a cord, but the sight of it made everyone smile, so she hadn't had the heart to replace it.

"Quilt Haus Inn. How may I help you?"

"My name is David. I work for Tri-County Suppliers. I have an invoice that says I'm supposed to pick up a return shipment heading to Carmichael Foods. I'm calling to make sure it's ready to go."

"Hold on one minute, please." Julie placed her hand over the receiver and addressed Hannah. "Do you have a return shipment for Carmichael Foods?"

She shook her head. "What's it for?"

Julie uncapped the phone. "I'm sorry, we don't have a record of this. Can you give me more details?"

"Yes ma'am. It says here that there's been a factory recall on their vegetable oil. Seems it's been contaminated with peanut oil and needs to be returned."

Julie sighed with relief as she made her way to her office.

After putting Hannah on the phone with the trucking company and two calls to Carmichael Foods, the tainted oil was finally ready to be picked up. But the biggest relief came from knowing that Joyce's attack had been strictly accidental—not the work of a cold-blooded killer.

Now if they could only solve the mystery of who killed Alice and why, life would be perfect again. Or close to it.

She resisted the urge to check her watch and see how much longer everyone had to remain at the inn—a watched pot and all that. Instead, she went to her office and retrieved the journal from the safe.

She'd promised Aston Cooper, the book expert and museum curator, a look at the book. Now that it was back in her hands, she could make good on her promise. She took the non-flash pictures he'd requested and sent them to him via email from her cellphone. She was anxious to know what Aston thought. Something told her the book would be worth more than she was originally led to believe. It took everything she had not to drum her fingers against her desk in her impatience.

Her phone dinged, and she snatched it off the desk. The message was from Aston: "I'll get back to you as soon as I know something."

"Julie?" She turned as Shirley poked her head into the office. "Daniel Franklin's here."

"Tell him to come on back."

"I already did," Shirley said. "But he said he'd wait for you out front."

"Thanks, Shirley. I'll be right out."

"I'll let him know." The redhead disappeared.

Julie locked the journal inside the safe, turning the dial to make sure the tumblers set correctly. She wasn't about to take any chances. Running her hands through her long hair to try and tame any wayward curls, she headed to the front of the inn.

"Daniel," Julie greeted him as she stepped into the front hall. "What brings you by today?"

He smiled. "You."

She wasn't sure how to respond to that, but ignoring the slight flutter of her pulse seemed like a good start. "Me?"

"I think you need a break from all this craziness."

She was shaking her head before he even finished. "I can't leave today."

"Come with me and get a cup of coffee. We're talking an hour max."

"I don't know, Daniel."

"Give me one good reason."

"The guests are all still here, for one thing."

"So? They're big people; they can do without you for one little hour."

"But—"

He shook his head, smiling that charming smile that showed off his irresistible dimples. "The place is not going to fall apart if you leave for a while."

"How sure are you about that?"

"One hundred percent positive." There was that smile again. "You need a break from all of the stress in this place. I'm here to make sure you get it."

"You're not going to give up, are you?" she asked.

"Not a chance."

Julie could almost feel her hair curling as she and Daniel stepped into the humidity. She cast a glance back at the old mansion as they walked down the sidewalk. It was such a beautiful house with its big windows, deep red color, and turrets reaching toward the sky.

"Café Bona?" Daniel asked. It was the best place in Straussberg to get a cup of coffee, though their pastries weren't nearly as tasty as Hannah's.

"Lead the way."

A few minutes later, he pointed to one of the cheerful umbrella-covered tables lining the walk. "You sit. I'll go get us something."

Julie complied.

It felt good to be out in the open air and not shut up with a group of strangers, including a possible killer. She propped her elbow on the tabletop, rested her chin in her hand, and raised her face toward the sky. Closing her eyes, she let the golden rays of the sun wash over her.

"You look more relaxed already." Daniel's deep voice pulled her back to reality.

Julie smiled and opened her eyes as he took a seat opposite her, handing her a steaming mug of coffee and a piece of lemon cake.

"Thanks," she said.

"I know their desserts aren't on par with Hannah's, but you needed to get out."

"You're right," she said. "On both accounts."

He laughed and took a sip of his coffee. "Wish I had that on tape."

They shared a smile. Then she looked away.

"Anything interesting happen today?" he asked.

"I found the journal."

"What?" Daniel sat up straight. "Where was it?"

Julie proceeded to fill him in on recent events.

"Unbelievable," Daniel said. "Kenneth must lead a terribly boring life. Who knew podiatrists were so strange?"

"They do play with feet all day. Thankfully, everything was pretty quiet when I left. The guests were in the tearoom, playing cards and quilting. Here's hoping it stays that way." Julie raised her coffee cup and they drank to that.

"Have you heard anything from the police? Do they have any idea who might have wanted Alice dead?"

"No." Julie sighed. "They've talked to each guest at various points throughout the weekend—discreetly, in person, and by phone. But to my knowledge, they have no solid leads."

"I'm sorry to hear that." Daniel paused. "And what about you?"

"What about me?"

He cocked a brow. "Don't play coy. I know you've been doing some investigating of your own."

She pursed her lips but didn't deny it.

"Do you have any leads?" he pressed.

"Nothing concrete. Only what Carrie told me she saw the night the lights went out. If only she'd gotten a good look at the person holding the book. I'm certain that's our murderer—one of them, at least. There could be two people working together for all I know."

"I don't like this," Daniel said, the worry evident in his eyes.

"That makes two of us," Julie said. "Nine o'clock tonight can't come soon enough."

He lifted his cup in salute. "To nine."

She raised her mug to clink with his, but before she could complete the action, a movement across the street caught her attention. *Sadie.*

"So *that's* where she disappeared to," she muttered to herself, watching her walk down the sidewalk.

"Who?" Daniel started to turn, but Julie ducked down, pulling Daniel sideways and underneath the table with her.

"Shhh," she said.

"You mind telling me what's going on?" he asked, his nose inches from hers.

"Sadie Davidson is over there, across the street." Julie watched as Sadie glanced nervously from one side to the other and then looked behind her as if she were being followed. She carried her big white handbag looped over one arm as she hustled down the sidewalk, neatly darting through the milling tourists. The woman suddenly appeared very spry for her age.

"I thought you said everyone was in the tearoom," Daniel said.

"I did," she hissed in return. "I meant everyone except for Sadie. And Gregory."

"And why are we under the table?" Daniel contorted his head around to peer at the older woman. "And it better be a good reason because this is killing my back."

"Because I don't want her to see me here."

"Why not?" He pulled against her hold. "You do live here after all."

"Because we're going to follow her."

"That's an interesting notion." He pulled harder and broke free of her grasp so he could sit up straight in his seat. They'd garnered more than a few curious looks from the folks around them. "Why are we going to follow her?"

"Because she's acting weird." Julie sat up in her seat.

"So are you."

"*I* wasn't the one who left my self-proclaimed 'bestie' all alone at the hospital in a strange town after she nearly died." Julie grabbed the menu off the table and held it front of her face with one hand as she gathered her purse. "Are you with me or not, Franklin?"

Daniel sighed, but his eyes sparkled with the light of rekindled adventure. "How could I possibly resist?"

They walked together down the street, doing their best to stay out of Sadie's peripheral vision while not losing sight of her. It helped that the older woman was on the opposite side of the street, but Julie wasn't taking any chances.

"Something weird is going on with her," Julie said. "Why else would she leave Joyce at the hospital?"

"Maybe to enjoy the rest of her vacation."

"Really?" She cast an annoyed glance at Daniel.

"Just a guess," he replied.

"The two women seemed closer than that." Julie glanced across the street again, but Sadie was nowhere to be seen. "We've lost her!"

They stopped and scanned the entire street. As usual, there were a lot of people milling about the town, tourists and locals alike.

"There she is." Daniel pointed just ahead of them.

As Sadie crossed the street and came toward them, Julie grabbed Daniel's shirt and dragged him into the alcove of a nearby store entrance.

Sadie's sweet-sounding voice drifted their way as she hurried past their hiding spot, her phone to her ear. "...missing ... must have a master plan ... now I'm getting worried. ..."

"Did you hear that?" Julie said. "I can't believe she's involved in any of this!"

"Bits and pieces—don't jump to conclusions." Daniel fixed a stern look on her. "She could've been talking about anything. That short conversation doesn't prove her guilt."

"Yeah—and I'm the tooth fairy. Do you think she spotted us?"

"No."

Julie peered around Daniel just in time to see Sadie dart into the hardware store. "Not guilty, huh? What would Sadie possibly need from the hardware store during her vacation?"

Daniel shrugged. "Maybe she's getting a new lock for her suitcase."

"Or buying more tools to put in her handbag so she can *pretend* to be afraid."

"What?"

Julie explained how everyone had started carrying around some form of makeshift weapon.

"Did you tell the detective about that?" Daniel asked.

"Detective Frost! Oh, gosh," Julie said, fishing her phone out of her purse. "I completely forgot to tell him that we found the journal."

"How could you forget to tell him something like that?"

Julie put a hand on her hip. "In my defense, there has been a lot going on lately."

"OK, I'll let you have that one."

"It's him!" Julie exclaimed, pointing across the street.

"Him who?"

"That man. I remember who he is now."

"Care to enlighten me?" Daniel asked, his gaze following her outstretched finger.

"Eric Rutherford." Julie watched the man on the sidewalk through narrowed eyes. "He came into the inn the other day at the peak of the chaos. He looked familiar to me then, but I couldn't place him. And I really didn't have time to dwell on it. But I know it's Rutherford, I saw his picture online."

"Back up. Who's Eric Rutherford?" Daniel asked.

Julie looked from Rutherford to the hardware store Sadie had disappeared into and then back to Daniel. "He was Alice Peyton's boss and the book expert I called first."

Daniel frowned. "The one who told you the book was practically worthless."

"The very same," Julie said, unsure of whom to follow—Sadie or Rutherford. Before she could decide, her phone rang. "It's the inn," she said, peering at the screen. "Something must have happened. Hello?"

"Julie!" Shirley exclaimed through the phone. "You need to come see this. Right *now*."

"What happened?"

"Just hurry!" Shirley disconnected before Julie could press her for details.

Julie looked at Daniel. "There's some kind of emergency at the inn. I have to go back."

"Another one?" Daniel said.

Julie sighed as she watched Rutherford slip away. "My sentiments exactly."

Shirley met them outside as they rounded the street corner near the inn.

"Oh, Julie," Shirley lamented. "This is terrible, just terrible!"

"Calm down and tell me what's happened."

The redhead pressed her lips together and shook her head. "You have to come see it for yourself."

She pulled on Julie's hand, leading the way up the steps and into the mansion.

"*Look.*" Shirley took Julie by the shoulders and turned her toward the far wall of the front sitting area. It was normally a cozy little nook with comfy chairs, good lighting, and a warm ambiance. But not today. Not with the menacing words that were spray-painted across the wall and furniture.

Stunned, Julie read the words aloud. "Alice is dead. I'm coming for it."

The person responsible for the unsightly graffiti obviously hadn't cared about anything other than getting that message across. The thick black letters covered everything in their path. The exclamation point ended on the overstuffed armchair. The paintings on the walls, the window frame ... nothing had been spared.

"Whoa," Daniel said, whistling under his breath.

"How could this happen?" Julie asked.

Shirley wrung her hands and looked like she was about to burst into tears. "I really used to love this place, but now … it's like a never-ending bad dream."

Julie wrapped an arm around Shirley and pulled her in close. "It's OK, Shirley. This is still a good place. Somehow we've managed to attract the wrong kind of guest this week, that's all."

Shirley attempted a shaky smile, but she still appeared dubious.

"Where is everyone?" Julie asked.

"Liam went to work on his book. Carrie said since it wasn't raining any longer, she was going out into the garden. I have no idea about Gregory or Sadie. Susan and Kenneth went to lie down."

Julie furrowed her brows. "Kenneth shouldn't be sleeping with that head injury."

Shirley nodded and pulled a crumpled tissue from her pocket to dab at the corners of her eyes. "I promised I would wake him in an hour."

"When did you find this?" Julie pointed at the offensive message.

"Just a little bit ago."

Daniel went to the wall and touched the paint, pulling back his fingers to examine them. "It's dry," he said, showing them his clean hand.

"Have you called the police?" Julie asked.

"Not yet," Shirley said. "I thought you should see it first."

After phoning the police, Daniel ducked into Julie's office to look at the Civil War journal and pass the time while Julie worked at the front desk, waiting for the police. It didn't take long. Julie suspected Detective Frost was on permanent standby, waiting for something else to go wrong at the inn. A sure testimony to this fact was that he arrived before the uniforms did.

"Detective Frost." Julie greeted him from her perch behind the desk as he let himself in the front door.

"Miss Ellis. I'm beginning to think I should rent a room here to save on gas." He turned to inspect the words splattered across the wall and furnishings. "When you make someone angry, you sure do it up right."

"All or nothing." She shrugged.

"Any possible witnesses to this one?" The detective took a penlight out of his trouser pocket and shone it toward the crudely painted letters.

"Not that I'm aware of. I was gone when it happened. Shirley found it."

"Shirley, huh?"

"Yes." Julie didn't like his tone. "Did you find out any more about Alice from her family?"

He gave her a "Nice try" smile and put the tiny light back into his pocket. "No more than I'm sure you found out on the Internet."

Julie pursed her lips. Clearly he had no intention of discussing the case with her. "It would be helpful if someone could at least determine why she lied about her marital status and who bought her trip to Straussberg."

"Where are all the guests today?" he asked.

"Carrie's in the garden. Liam, Susan, and Kenneth are upstairs in their rooms."

"What about that other fellow? Gregory, was it?"

"He's made himself scarce this morning," Julie said.

"Does that seem odd to you?"

Julie chuckled. "Most everything about the man seems odd to me. But at least it's been more peaceful around here with him gone."

"Hmmm." The detective said it in a way that could mean almost anything.

Shirley sashayed down the hall toward them. "Sadie just called. They're waiting on the doctor to release Joyce, and then they're coming back here."

That still doesn't explain Sadie's trip to the hardware store.

Shirley glanced at her watch. "It's been an hour. I'd better go wake Kenneth or we might have more trouble." She hustled past them in a flurry of flowing bright fabrics.

"Why would Kenneth give you trouble?" Frost's brown eyes pinned Julie again.

Julie pressed her lips together but then decided there was no sense in hiding it from Frost. "Liam accidently hit him in the head with a lamp."

The detective's brows shot up. "Assault?"

"No, no, no. It was an everyday sort of accident."

"Right." Frost scribbled another note on his pad.

"But the really good news is we found out that the cooking oil company is responsible for Joyce's exposure to peanuts," Julie added quickly. "So, no one tried to poison Joyce. Isn't that fantastic?"

He didn't look impressed by the news.

"Oh! And we found the journal," she said.

"Where was it?" Frost drawled. "In your purse?"

Julie bit back a sharp retort and launched into the story. Detective Frost put on his business face and scribbled in his notebook as another officer came in.

"You again?" the young officer said to Julie.

Julie shrugged good-naturedly. "What can I say?"

Detective Frost filled him in on the particulars, set him to writing the report, and then turned back to Julie. "So, you have no idea who's responsible for this?"

"I didn't say that."

Frost sighed with exasperation. "You mean we've been standing around here gabbing for half an hour, and all the while you've known who did this?"

"I was answering your questions."

Detective Frost put his notepad away and folded his arms across his broad chest. "OK, Miss Ellis. Will you kindly enlighten me as to whom you think spray-painted that threat on your property?"

"I'd be happy to," she said with a small grin. "It was Alice's killer."

FIFTEEN

Detective Frost stared at Julie like he wanted to strangle her. "Do you find this amusing, Miss Ellis?" he asked.

"Not at all," she replied, wiping the grin off her face. "Quite the opposite, in fact. I find the situation ghastly. But I'm being honest. It's clear to me that Alice's killer did this." She waved a hand toward the graffiti on the wall. "And it's obviously someone who has easy access to the inn."

"Thank you for spelling that out for me," Frost said, pulling out his notepad again. He walked closer to the wall to study it. "What's interesting is that the perp doesn't say 'I'm coming after *you*,'" Detective Frost pointed out. "He says, 'it.' 'I'm coming after it.' Any idea what this is in reference to?"

"The only thing I can think of would be the old Civil War journal. News of it made the papers. Someone must think it's more valuable than it really is." Julie paused. "And then there's Eric Rutherford."

"Who's that?"

"Alice Peyton's boss."

That brought Frost to attention.

"Julie," Daniel called. From the sound of his voice, he was standing in her office doorway. "You might want to come take a look at this."

No. No, I don't.

"Excuse me for a moment, please," Julie said to the detective. She quickly made her way to her office.

"You are not going to believe this," Daniel started, opening the Civil War journal. "Look here." He pointed at the page and then began to read. "'Becky is new in town, but Tom loves her.

He wants them to become engaged. One kiss ought to do it.'"

It took a moment for what Daniel read to sink in. *Becky, Tom* ... "You don't mean ...?"

Daniel smiled and flipped back to the front. He pointed to the inscription written in a spidery, slanted scrawl. "Property of SLC 1861."

"Samuel Langhorne Clemens," she whispered in awe.

Daniel nodded, the grin on his face wider than the Mississippi River that Clemens so artfully wrote about. "We would need to have it authenticated, but it sure looks legit to me," he said.

Julie picked up the book and held it in her hands, staring at it in wonder. Of all the treasures she had ever recovered in her previous life of antiquities bounty hunting, this one seemed truly special. Perhaps because she could trace it back to an American icon. Everyone knew who Mark Twain was. "Do you think it really was his?"

"The dates fit. Clemens volunteered for the war in 1861. He only served for two weeks before his company disbanded."

Behind her, Detective Frost whistled. "Sorry. Couldn't help but overhear. That sure is something."

Gently, Julie thumbed through the pages. Not all were written on and not all of the writing was legible. A handwriting expert would have to be called to authenticate the ownership, but all the signs pointed to one thing: The book had belonged to one of the greatest American writers of all time.

"I can't donate this to the auction," Julie said.

"That's what I've been trying to tell you," Daniel said. "But don't let your hopes get too high. It could turn out to be nothing. Or some kind of hoax."

True. She'd spent enough time in the art business to know the world was full of fakes and reproductions. The book she'd found could be nearly priceless or not even worth the paper it was written on. But she had a feeling this was the real deal, and she was usually right about these sorts of things.

"I'm sure Aston can help us out with that," Julie said.

"Who's Aston?" Frost asked.

"A book expert. I emailed him pictures of some pages he requested this morning."

The detective nodded. "Be sure to let me know what he says. I'd like to talk to your staff and guests, and I plan to check into this Eric Rutherford fellow too." He walked out of the office and made his way back to the front of the inn with Julie trailing behind. "In the meantime, I suggest you do your best to fly under the radar and stop making people angry."

"Thanks for the tip," Julie said with a wry smile. If she knew how to do that, she would have started a long time ago.

After talking to the guests in residence and Hannah, Detective Frost took pictures of the wall and told Julie to call if she saw anything else suspicious.

"I'd give you my card," he said on his way out, "but you already have one."

Sometime around three, Sadie arrived at the inn with a pale-looking Joyce in tow.

"Oh dear, I'm so happy to see you." Joyce grabbed Julie for an uncomfortable hug. "I've been so worried that you would be mad at me."

Julie disentangled herself from the woman's embrace. Joyce was surprisingly strong for a woman who had been two steps from death's door the night before.

"Why would I be upset with you?" Julie asked.

"For ruining the weekend."

Julie bit her lip to keep from laughing at the absurd statement. "You did no such thing."

"Is the quilt finished?" Joyce asked.

"No—and speaking of that," Julie said, "we have a little more work to do on it. I was hoping I could get all quilting hands on deck in the tearoom to try and finish it up."

"That sounds lovely, dear," Sadie said.

They found Carrie, Susan, and Liam already in the tearoom, hard at work on the quilt. Kenneth sat close by, entertaining himself with a cheater's game of solitaire.

"What did we miss?" Joyce asked as she settled down next to Carrie.

Shirley's eyes twinkled as she started the new tale of what all happened after Joyce had gone to the hospital, including Liam clunking Kenneth on the back of the head, the plot of the murder mystery, and the return of the Civil War journal.

"And then the company called and said that the oil Hannah used for the oven-fried chicken Saturday night was contaminated with peanuts. That's what caused your reaction—not a crazed killer."

"Oh." Joyce almost sounded disappointed by the news.

"I'll have Hannah get you their number. I'm sure there's a lawsuit brewing on this one already," Shirley said.

Joyce waved a dismissive hand. "I don't want to sue anyone. I'm all right. And it was an accident."

Julie could hardly believe the graciousness of the lady. They didn't make them like her anymore.

Joyce sighed. "I have a confession to make though." She twisted her mouth this way and that as if the contortions would help her say what needed to be said. "I don't quilt. I've always wanted to learn, but I never did. When Sadie mentioned coming here for the weekend, I was so excited to get away that I never gave it a second thought until that first day when someone gave me a needle. I'm so very sorry that I deceived you. I never meant any harm."

Susan patted her arm reassuringly. "That's all right. Kenneth doesn't really quilt either."

Everyone laughed.

Everyone but Kenneth. "I'll have you know I make nice, even stitches," he huffed.

"Well, you *are* a doctor," Carrie said wisely.

"What about you, Dr. Preston?" Joyce asked with a wicked twinkle in her eye. "Are you really a quilter, or did you come here under false pretenses as well?"

"A little of both," Liam said without a hint of apology in his voice. "My parents died when I was eight. My grandmother raised me, and she was an avid quilter. Every time I pick up a needle and thread, I can't help but think of her."

Joyce reached over and patted him on the cheek. "You are a good boy," she said. "Even if you did lie about your name."

Liam blinked several times, noticeably at a loss for a reply.

Joyce chuckled. "My dear man, did you think you had any of us fooled?"

"Well, I ..."

"Clearly you feel that we aren't your audience and therefore wouldn't have bought your books or seen your picture," Sadie said.

Liam looked like he had been hit by a bus. "Does everyone here know who I am?" he finally asked.

They all nodded.

"And no one said anything?"

"I thought the ruse was rather exciting," Joyce said.

"In all fairness, Liam Preston *is* my name. Liam Preston Wallis—L.P. for short."

Julie looked to Carrie. The girl had her head bent so low over the quilt that Julie didn't know how she could possibly see. Julie never had finished her research, but to think that the young girl was anything more than a poor college student seemed wrong somehow. But even after Liam's confession, Carrie remained closemouthed.

"Did anyone see today's paper?" Shirley asked. "That cute little pop star disappeared."

"Which singer?" Susan asked.

"CeCe," Shirley said.

"Disappeared?" Liam asked.

"Evidently, she went into her bus on Thursday night, crawled through the window while everyone was asleep, and disappeared. Her manager is fit to be tied. I guess her family is pretty concerned too."

"Joyce called me from the hospital earlier and told me about it. I love CeCe's music," Sadie said. She bounced a little in her seat as if a pop song were playing in her head. "I'm sure she'll reappear when she's ready. It's probably all part of a master marketing plan."

Julie realized that what she'd overheard Sadie talking about when she and Daniel were following the woman may well have been related to the singer's disappearing act—not the murder.

"Didn't she win that television show *The Singer*?" Susan asked.

"Year before last," Shirley nodded. "Then the article said she spent a couple of months in the studio, recording an album, and she's been on tour ever since."

"Do they still call them 'albums'?" Kenneth asked.

"Yes dear," Susan said without looking up from her stitches.

"It's a legitimate question, given all the changes in the music industry these days," he said defensively.

Sadie and Joyce nodded as if they kept current on all the new technological advances in the music world.

Julie listened to the chatter. This—*this*—was what she had imagined the weekend would be like. Sipping coffee, telling stories, peace and quiet. No murders or snakes or vandalism.

And still no Gregory. She almost hated to ask about him. The lack of drama was one thing, but without her sourpuss guest there, complaining every step of the way, the peace took on a whole new level of tranquility. Still, she wished she knew where he was. Especially after the threat that had been left on the sitting-room wall. "Has anyone seen Gregory?"

"I'm right here." The man in question sauntered into the room.

"Would you like to sit down here, dear?" Sadie asked, patting the seat next to her.

Gregory shook his head.

Where had he been all day? Julie wanted to ask, but for once, he wasn't complaining, and she thought it best to let it slide for the moment.

"We were just talking about pop stars and quilting," Sadie said to him, not one bit offended that he refused her offer of a place to sit down. "How did you become a quilter?"

"I'm not really a quilter," Gregory confessed without an ounce of shame.

Julie knew taking that ad out in the mystery magazine had been a mistake. And here was additional proof.

"But I paid my way through college working in a tailor shop and then doing car upholstery," Gregory added.

"Really?" Joyce asked. "How interesting." She had joined Kenneth at the card table and was trying to make him play fair. "If you didn't come here to quilt, that must mean you're a mystery buff."

He shrugged. "Yeah. And I needed to get away for a while. My life's been hectic lately."

Julie narrowed her eyes at him. If he needed to get away so badly, why had he waited to reserve his room until the very last minute? And how had he managed to time his phone call just right and snap up the late cancellation?

Crazy coincidence. That's what it had to be. If he were after the journal, he'd have made his reservation earlier.

Thinking about the old book made Julie want to spring from her seat and check the office safe to make sure it was still there. She'd asked Daniel to lock it in the safe when he left, but she hadn't actually seen him do it.

Now I'm being paranoid. The journal is safe and sound.

At the moment, she had an inn full of guests, a murderer on the loose, a potential vandal, and a house full of probable liars. She glanced over at Kenneth. As soon as Joyce turned her head, he shuffled the deck to get better cards to the top of the draw pile.

He gave Joyce an innocent smile as she turned back around.

Julie didn't know whether to laugh or cry.

SIXTEEN

To say that dinner was a strained affair that evening would be the understatement of the year.

Hannah had made a pasta-and-shrimp dish (after double-checking to make sure no one had a problem with shellfish), a salad of spring greens, and homemade French rolls with fresh butter.

It should have been satisfying and wonderful, the perfect ending to a not-so-perfect weekend. But hateful looks were thrown about like daggers, and frowns reigned as the expression of choice.

"This is fun," Daniel whispered dryly to Julie. He'd come over so they could look at the journal together later in the evening—after the guests left. Julie was glad to have him in her camp.

She took a drink of water and tried to act as if everything were normal. Wine from one of the local vineyards had been served, but she limited herself to half a glass so she'd be better prepared for … anything. She looked around at the guests. What an interesting, colorful bunch of people. Despite all of their many quirks, she really couldn't imagine any of them being a murderer. Even Carrie had somehow wormed her way into Julie's heart. Oh, she knew the young girl still had secrets, but those were hers to keep. Secrets didn't make someone a criminal. Everyone had secrets.

Yet, the fact remained that one of them was likely a killer. There was no other logical explanation for the weekend's events.

"Did you have a good day today, Gregory?" she asked, hoping for a clue as to where he had been.

At the sound of her voice, everyone looked up and then looked at Gregory.

"I suppose." He glared at her as if she'd crossed some imaginary line with the question.

She would not be deterred. "Did you do a lot of sightseeing?"

He shrugged.

"Where did you go?" she asked as innocently as possible.

"I don't have to tell you that. You're nothing but a busybody. Why do you always eat with us anyway? It's weird."

Carrie gasped at his outburst.

"You are rude." Daniel pointed his fork at Gregory for emphasis.

"And?" Gregory tossed down his napkin. "I've had enough of this. Why don't you ask everyone else where they were today, dear innkeeper?"

With tremendous willpower, Julie kept her tone civil. "OK. Sadie, I saw you in town today. Did you have a nice time?"

"It was lovely," Sadie said, her voice quiet and subdued. Not at all the Sadie of the past few days.

"Yes, the hardware store is lovely this time of year," Gregory sneered. "Did you get all the paint you needed?"

The room fell completely silent, and a few forks paused in midair.

"Are you accusing Sadie of painting that ghastly threat on the wall?" Joyce's voice was barely above a whisper.

Gregory only shrugged, but his expression spoke volumes.

"Sadie wouldn't do something like that," Carrie said, her face turning bright pink. "She's a sweet little lady."

"Thank you, dear," Sadie said.

"You're only saying that because she has one of your songs as her ringtone," Kenneth said slyly. "And for the record, I also find it odd that Sadie went to the hardware store. If it's true."

The room fell silent again for one split second, and then the chaos erupted.

Carrie stood and acted as if she were going to leave. Then she sat back down again and pulled off her glasses, tossing them aside. "Fine. You're right. I'm not who I'm pretending to be."

"I thought you looked familiar!" Susan exclaimed. "Kenneth, why didn't you tell me?" She smacked him on the arm.

Liam was frantically taking notes on one of the napkins. "Golden," he muttered. "Better than fiction."

"You mean all this time …" Joyce's eyes grew wide with surprise. "Sadie," she said, elbowing her companion. "That's CeCe! That's the singer who disappeared from her tour bus."

"I know." Sadie dug into her purse. She pulled out a Taser and set it on the table in front of her before digging out a piece of paper and a pen.

"Whoa!" Kenneth stood and put his hands into the air as he stepped in front of his wife. "There's no need to get out your gun. We're all friends here. And I take back the hardware store comment."

"This old thing?" Sadie picked up the weapon and turned it over in her hands. "This will only stun you. The real gun is in the car. And for the record, I stopped into the hardware store to get a new battery for my Taser."

Julie swallowed hard. "You have a gun with you?"

"Of course, dear. Two women traveling alone. You can't be too careful, you know." Sadie chuckled. "Well, I suppose if you didn't know this before, you certainly do after what's happened here this weekend."

"Right," Julie murmured, eyeing the Taser.

Sadie tucked the weapon away and then handed the paper and pen to Carrie. "Will you autograph this for me, dear? Write, 'To my biggest fan, Sadie Jane Davidson.'"

Carrie took the paper like it was contaminated but quickly signed it and handed it back.

Sadie beamed.

"Carrie—CeCe—we're thrilled you've come to stay with us," Julie said. "But what happened? Why are you here?"

Carrie sighed. "I just needed a break from all the craziness, you know?"

Julie certainly did.

"The newspaper said you climbed out the bus window," Shirley prompted.

Julie wondered how much story mileage Shirley would be able to get out of having the incomparable CeCe in her humble tearoom.

"That's right," Carrie said. "I climbed out the window with the clothes on my back and some cash in my pocket. The first stop I made was to cut the extensions out of my hair. I knew they would give me away for sure. And I tried to soak my acrylic nails off, but I grew impatient and ended up tearing a few." Which explained why her hands looked like they had been chewed on by angry beavers.

"That wasn't your real hair?" Sadie seemed overly disappointed at that fact.

"Hardly anyone in Hollywood has real hair anymore," Carrie said.

Sadie frowned. "Oh."

"Then I went by a thrift store and bought some clothes, including that prom dress and these ridiculous glasses," Carrie continued. "And you know the rest."

As Julie listened, everything started to click into place. Why Carrie kept running into walls and stumbling. Why her clothes looked like they belonged to someone else. And why she seemed determined to blend into the woodwork. But surprise, surprise, their little wallflower was a big pop star.

"I know it sounds selfish, but I don't regret coming here. Even with everything that's happened." Carrie shrugged. "It's actually much more relaxing here than on tour."

Everyone laughed.

"Am I the only one who cares that there was a murder here and the culprit is about to get away with it?" Susan's shrill voice cut through the room like a knife. She looked at each one of them in turn. "Or do you only care about spray paint and singers?"

"That's not fair." Carrie shook her head, her lips pressed together.

"Who said any part of this weekend was going to be fair?" Gregory said.

"Life rarely is," Kenneth agreed.

"Someone was *murdered*." Susan drew out the last word, somehow making it three syllables.

"I say we just forget the whole thing," Gregory said. "Stop bringing it up. Quit talking about it. Whoever killed Alice obviously had their reasons. We should let sleeping dogs lie, and everyone goes home safe and sound."

"Everyone but Alice," Carrie tossed in. "How can you be so cold?"

"*Murdered*," Susan repeated.

"So, you're suggesting we simply try to forget it?" Kenneth asked with a scoff. "Act like it didn't happen? Wait until the detective gets here and then merrily go home?"

"Why not?" Gregory shrugged. "You got any better ideas? It would keep things a lot more pleasant around this place."

Julie couldn't remain quiet any longer. "That is the most ridiculous plan I have ever heard."

"I second that."

Everyone turned as Detective Frost entered the room. With all the commotion, Julie hadn't heard the bell over the door ring.

"You're early, Detective," Julie said. "Would you like to join us?"

"I came to talk to a couple of you again."

Murmurs buzzed around the table. But all of the expressions proclaimed innocence. No one was giving away anything.

The detective turned his hawklike eyes toward the doctor. "Kenneth Calhoun."

Kenneth stood and stretched his legs. Susan looked as if she were going to cry.

"I wonder what *that's* all about," Joyce whispered after the two men left the room to talk in the hall.

"That cop." Gregory shook his head. "He's trying to intimidate us. Make somebody crack." He looked at each of them in turn as if watching for a sign of weakness. "I guess there's no way we can pretend it didn't happen with *him* here."

Susan bit her lip, obviously trying to hear what was going on in the hall. Everyone else picked at their key lime pie. After what seemed like an eternity of Gregory glaring at everyone in the room, Kenneth returned.

"I hope you saved a piece for me," he said as he took his seat.

Susan wilted with relief.

Julie couldn't help but wonder why the woman had been so worried. What did she know?

Detective Frost stopped at the door and looked to tiny Carrie Windsor, also known as CeCe the Pop Star. "Miss Windsor?"

Carrie looked at Sadie and Joyce as if somehow they could help her. Both of the older women promptly dropped their gazes to their pie.

"Coming." Carrie pushed to her feet and followed the detective into the hall.

Gregory turned to Kenneth. "What'd he ask you?"

This time, Liam dropped all pretense of merely paying attention and pulled out a notebook, pen poised and ready to write.

"Nothing he hasn't already asked before," Kenneth said, but Julie knew he was lying.

She looked to Daniel, who gave a small shrug. Then he pushed a piece of paper toward her with a note scrawled on it.

"What if there really are two?"

Two *what*? Julie studied his face, and his meaning finally registered. Two people involved in the murder. She hadn't put much stock in the theory before.

But what if there *were* two criminals under her roof?

It was eight-thirty by the time Detective Frost escorted Carrie back into the room. She looked calm enough, as if she'd just had a talk with a good friend instead of a hardened detective on a mission.

"Time's up," Frost said, looking around the faces in the room.

"So that's it?" Gregory asked. "We're free to go?"

The detective nodded. "For now. But we may need to contact you in the near future as we continue the investigation. I expect you all to answer the phone when we call. I guarantee you it will make things easier for everyone if you do."

"It's about time." Gregory stood and stalked out the door, presumably to pack his bags and get out of town. The tension in the room dropped after he was gone, but it didn't go away completely.

"Would it be OK if we stayed until tomorrow?" Sadie asked

Julie. "It'll be dark soon, and I don't like driving in the dark."

Joyce nodded her head in emphasis to her friend's words.

"Of course," Julie said. "We don't have many bookings this week, so you're in luck."

Liam was already staying as were Susan and Kenneth. Julie felt her hopes about the dreadful weekend drawing to a close soon slip away. Half of her guests weren't leaving when they were supposed to.

"What about you, dear?" Sadie asked Carrie. "Can you stay one more night with us?"

Suddenly the girl seemed very interested in her own fingernails. "I have my room booked for the whole week, but I don't think I can stay."

"You should call your manager," Joyce said. "You have people missing you and wondering if you're all right."

Carrie nodded.

Sadie patted the girl's knee. "You tell them you have people who are watching out for you. They can come and get you tomorrow, but for now you need one more night of rest."

Carrie sighed. "I guess it's about time I went back to my real life."

Julie smiled reassuringly. "You can come hide out here anytime you want."

Carrie's eyes lit up like she'd been given the best gift on the planet. "You really mean that?"

Julie nodded, surprised the girl would even entertain the thought after the weekend they'd had. "You'll always have a room here."

Upon hearing it all, Detective Frost left, shaking his head as he went.

"I know Aston Cooper will be here tomorrow to check out the journal," Daniel said as Julie unlocked the safe and took out the book. "But this can't wait until then." His eyes sparkled, and his hands shook with excitement.

"I can tell," she replied with a laugh.

Daniel opened the book to the title page. "This is no ordinary book."

"I thought we covered this," Julie said. "It might have belonged to Mark Twain."

"It's a manual on how to play baseball."

"Baseball?"

"Yeah." Daniel grinned.

"Was it even a sport in 1861?" Julie searched her brain for everything she knew about baseball. There wasn't much.

"It was a new game then. People were just starting to play it at the beginning of the Civil War. Some regiments received pocket manuals on all the rules."

"But the notes in the margins?"

"Pure Mark Twain."

"And this makes it more valuable?" Julie asked.

"There aren't a whole lot of these left. The game evolves, you know. Rules change, and things like this get destroyed. It's sad, really."

"Yes," she murmured. So much history tossed aside for the sake of advancement. "So, you're saying once we get this authenticated as belonging to Mark Twain, there's no telling what it'll be worth."

"I'm saying it will definitely be one of a kind," Daniel said. "And one-of-a-kind items are generally worth a lot."

Julie stared at the leather-bound book. Everything was falling into place, except ..."It really bothers me that we still don't know who the killer is."

"Of course it does," Daniel said. "It's your nature. It bothers me too."

Julie regarded him with curiosity. "About that note you wrote at dinner, when you said 'two,' I assume you didn't mean Sadie and Joyce."

"Nope." Daniel sat down in the chair behind her desk.

"Who then?"

"Eric Rutherford, for one."

"But how did he get in that night?" Julie shook her head. "No, I don't think he killed Alice. In fact, her family said the two of them were dating. Why would he kill his girlfriend?"

"For starters, it's not an uncommon scenario. Relationships turn sour. People get jealous. Who knows?"

"I don't think so. That doesn't feel like the right answer in this case."

"But you do believe that she was here to steal the book," Daniel pressed.

"Yes. I think Alice came to steal the book for Rutherford, and someone else wanted it and killed her for it."

"And that person is most likely whoever Carrie met in the hallway Friday night."

"Right," Julie said. "Someone like … Gregory."

Daniel rubbed his chin. "Aside from his *charming* personality, what makes you say that?"

"I'm being serious. Hear me out." She tapped one finger against her jaw as she thought out loud. "Gregory was accused of stealing a rare baseball card years ago, right?"

"Right."

"So, he'd probably know the worth of an antique baseball manual, say, one from the Civil War."

"But the article that ran in the newspapers didn't say anything about the journal being a baseball rule book."

"No, but there were pictures," Julie said. "Anyone looking close enough could see that."

Daniel nodded. "Especially someone who specialized in baseball collecting."

"We've been looking at this all wrong. It wasn't someone interested in the fact that it could have belonged to Mark Twain. It was someone who wanted it for its value in the world of sports."

"You should call Detective Frost right now—before Gregory can get too far out of town."

Julie nodded and started for the phone.

"How about you sit back down instead," an unfamiliar voice drawled from the door.

Julie whirled around.

Eric Rutherford stood in the doorway of her office holding a handgun aimed at her chest. He indicated the book with his free hand. "I'll take that."

Daniel's frown deepened into a scowl. Despite the gun the newcomer held, the historian was reluctant to give up the book. "You killed Alice Peyton."

Rutherford looked like he might come unglued. "I didn't kill her! I loved her."

"Against her family's wishes," Julie added, trying to figure out how she and Daniel were possibly going to get out of the mess alive. "I understand they didn't care for you."

Rutherford made a face to show exactly what he thought about Alice's family. "We were planning to get married. That book was going to set us up for life."

Julie thought about the bitter, sour-faced Alice and tried to picture her in love with the crazed man holding them at gunpoint. Even though Julie knew they'd been a couple, the image didn't gel. But the emotion in the man's words did. "You sent Alice here to steal the book from me?" she asked.

"Who's going to suspect a middle-aged divorcée?"

"She wasn't divorced," Julie countered.

"You didn't know that."

True enough. Alice would have been the last person on the suspect list of thieves as far as Julie was concerned. She had no previous record.

"Other people know that I have the book," Julie said. "If you try to take it, they'll know you stole it."

"You of all people should know there are other markets to sell such valuable items, Miss Ellis. Markets where buyers aren't so stringent about details like proper ownership."

Someone did their homework.

Rutherford took a few steps forward and waved the gun at Daniel. "Now hand it over."

Julie caught Daniel's eye, and she could see his resolve slipping. It was a valuable book, but not worth getting killed over.

"You lied to me," Julie said, inching toward the phone. "You told me the book was nothing special."

He shrugged. "Did you really think I was going to tell you the real value of what you have here?"

"Well, yeah." Julie nodded. "You are a *consultant*, after all."

The man laughed. "It's worth a fortune. And I mean to have it. Hand it over now." He cocked the gun. "Before someone gets hurt."

"OK. We'll give you the book." Julie shot Daniel a pointed look. She would not allow him to get shot over a stupid book. "But will you at least tell me this: If you didn't kill Alice, who did?"

"I did."

Their gazes all swung to the doorway where Gregory stood, a gun trained on them—a gun larger and meaner looking than the one Rutherford held.

Julie held her breath. For a moment she thought Rutherford might try and shoot Gregory where he stood. The look in his eyes was pure evil and full of hate. Perhaps he was telling the truth about loving Alice after all.

"You can go ahead and toss that aside, Rutherford." Gregory motioned with his own weapon for Rutherford to throw his gun to the ground. "Or I can shoot you where you stand. Your choice."

The older man hesitated for a moment. Then Gregory cocked the gun and Rutherford pitched his aside, raising his hands in the air.

"Well, well. The infamous Ghost lives. If you wanted to steal the book so badly, why didn't you just take it? Why did you have to kill Alice?" Rutherford's voice was thick with emotion.

"Why did you send your beloved to do your dirty work?" Gregory sneered. "Never send a woman to do a man's job."

Julie bit her tongue to keep from responding to the comment. Her intended reply would only make the situation worse.

Rutherford moved toward Gregory but stopped when he received a gun in his face for his troubles.

"If she meant that much to you," Gregory said, "you should have left her at home and come yourself. Of course, I would have simply killed you instead of her, but no matter." He shrugged as if it were all in a day's work.

A shiver ran down Julie's spine. Rutherford had been a threat, but a mild one, all things considered. He was grief stricken and here to claim what didn't belong to him. But Gregory was apparently a stone-cold killer.

She looked at Daniel and saw his expression was grim. All traces of hope had disappeared. After everything they'd been through in their short time together, this was how they would meet their end—at the hands of a petty thief.

No. Julie felt renewed resolve building inside her.

Maybe if she could keep Gregory talking about Alice long enough, Rutherford would eventually crack. If he rushed Gregory, then Julie and Daniel might have time to disarm him. Or at the very least, be able to overpower Gregory while he was busy fending off Rutherford. It was a long shot, but it beat doing nothing and becoming Gregory's next victims. She highly doubted he'd let them live once he got the book.

"Why did you kill Alice?" she asked.

Gregory fixed her with a hard stare. "She knew who I was. And I knew why she was here."

"And you murdered her without so much as a second thought?"

Gregory gave another of his devil-may-care shrugs. "I didn't mean to kill her. It just happened. When the lights went out, I knew she was going to make her move. So I stopped her and made *my* move. If I hadn't run into that crazy blonde in the hallway, I would have been long gone with that book days ago."

"You were the one Carrie took the book from," Julie said.

Gregory let out a bark of laughter. "Is that what she told you? Please. I *dropped* the book, but when I returned for it, it was gone. Then the lights came back on, and I had to high-tail it to the dining room before anyone realized I'd been gone."

His story made about as much sense as the one Carrie had told. But Julie supposed the truth was in the voice of the teller.

"Now give it here." He reached for the book. Daniel reluctantly handed it to him. "And you," he pointed to Rutherford, "get over there with the rest of them."

Rutherford grudgingly did as he was told. They were quickly running out of options and time.

Surely Gregory won't shoot us all, Julie thought, praying she was right.

"I'm not really a killer," Gregory continued. "But I—"

"Julie, I need you to approve this order for the kitchen." In true Hannah form, she pushed her way into the office, only to stop dead in her tracks and stare at the gun that swung to face her.

SEVENTEEN

Everything seemed to happen at once.

Daniel lunged toward Gregory. Julie dove for his gun, grabbing his hand and twisting it up and back. Gregory yelped in pain, and his hand went slack. Julie quickly wrenched the weapon away.

Hannah squealed, spurred into motion by the attack. She jumped to one side as Rutherford pounced on Gregory. He knocked Gregory and Daniel to the ground. Daniel managed to roll away while Rutherford straddled a sputtering Gregory, wrapping both hands around his pudgy neck.

Hannah fell to the floor and crawled behind the desk.

Gregory turned blue in the face as Daniel tried unsuccessfully to pull Rutherford off of him. Julie didn't think he was trying very hard. She snatched up Rutherford's discarded gun and handed it to Hannah, who took it with trembling fingers.

Then Julie pointed Gregory's gun at the men.

"Enough!" she screamed.

Daniel gave up on Rutherford. He took the gun from Hannah, gave her his phone, and joined Julie.

Rutherford eyed Julie warily. With a frustrated groan, he released his grip on Gregory.

Alice's killer coughed and then rolled to one side and scrambled to his feet. He glared at Julie. "And what do you think you're going to do? Shoot us?"

"Don't tempt me." Julie looked to Hannah who was trying to dial with shaky hands. "911?"

"I'm on it," Hannah said, though her voice lacked its usual gusto.

Detective Frost scratched his head. "Never a dull moment around you, huh, Miss Ellis?"

"I do what I can," she said.

Daniel caught her eye and smiled.

Gregory Wilson had been taken away in handcuffs, growling the entire time about the journal and Julie's interference. He'd been charged with murder, robbery, attempted robbery, attempted murder, and a host of other things the detectives tacked on for good measure. Julie wasn't sure how many of the charges would actually stick, but one thing was certain: Gregory wasn't getting out of jail for a long, long time.

Eric Rutherford was taken away in a separate police car with his own list of charges including attempted murder and conspiracy to commit a felony.

With any luck, *now* things could return to normal. Julie thought perhaps if she kept telling herself that, it would eventually come true.

Detective Frost watched the two police cars that carried Rutherford and Gregory drive away. Then he turned back to where Julie stood on the steps next to Daniel. "It's a fantastic story, to be sure."

She nodded. "I suppose. Everyone wanted the Civil War journal, and they were willing to stop at nothing to get it."

"Clearly," the detective said with a shake of his head. "That must be some book."

"We'll find out tomorrow when the other expert arrives," Daniel said. Julie could tell from his tone that he had high hopes for the new assessment.

"Let me know," Frost said, heading toward his car. "And you might think about getting some kind of security system installed in this place. Especially if you plan on digging up more valuables from the basement."

Daniel looked at Julie. "No," he said, shaking a finger at her. "You're not allowed to go down there again. Ever."

All the remaining guests gathered in the tearoom for one last get-together before they went to bed—as if any of them would be able to sleep. Julie was so keyed up, she didn't think she'd be able to sleep for a week.

Carrie's manager arrived that evening to whisk her away to Dallas. "CeCe" had a concert there the next day, and a lot of work to do to get ready. Julie hoped that the young star found her happy medium between who she wanted to be and who everyone thought she should be. It was hard to live a double life. This Julie knew from experience.

The group decided that since Carrie had done the most work on the quilt, it should belong to her. The young girl was thrilled. Joyce and Sadie looked a little sad, but no one disputed that the young pop star was the most deserving of the handmade treasure.

After Carrie left, everyone went to bed. Unable to sleep, Julie lay in bed, staring up at the ceiling. She thought about texting Daniel to see if he was awake too, or even knocking on Liam's door to see if he wanted to play a midnight game of checkers. But Daniel had looked utterly worn out when he left. And if Liam was awake, he would certainly be typing away at his laptop.

She rolled over, punched her pillow, and closed her eyes once again. But they quickly popped back open as if they had a mind of their own.

With a frustrated growl, she threw back the covers. Maybe a glass of warm milk would help her sleep. Then again, with all the excitement she had been through over the last four days, it might take a gallon.

She wrapped her robe around her and padded down the two flights of stairs to the first floor.

The inn was quiet; not even the sounds of Kenneth's snores could be heard. Soft shades of moonlight spilled in through the windows, giving the grand Victorian inn an otherworldly glow. The threatening note had been painted over, and the ruined couch replaced. Everything was as it should be.

But if that was the case, then why did she still feel so antsy?

With a shake of her head, she continued toward the kitchen on nearly silent feet.

Warm milk. She'd never gone in for it before, but there was a first time for everything, or so they said. She retrieved the milk from the fridge and found a pan. If only she had some chocolate. Now *that* sounded good. Not necessarily a cure for insomnia, but tasty all the same.

"What are you doing up at this hour?" Hannah appeared in the doorway. Her glasses were firmly in place, not a trace of sleep in her eyes.

"I could ask you the same thing."

Hannah shrugged. "I couldn't sleep. All the excitement, I guess. I keep waiting for the other shoe to fall."

"No more shoes, just milk. You want some?" Julie held up the jug.

"Sure." Hannah slid onto a stool at the island and propped her chin in one hand.

Julie poured enough for them both and turned on the burner.

"I've never seen this domestic side of you," Hannah commented.

"I only let it out on special occasions." Julie winked at her friend who in turn rolled her eyes. "Do we have any chocolate to go in here?"

Hannah slipped off the stool and walked to the pantry. Then, instead of handing Julie the cocoa and sugar, she bumped her out of the way and took over.

Julie gave a half-hearted protest before taking Hannah's place at the island. "We don't happen to have any caramel?" she asked.

Hannah shot her a horrified look. "If you eat that at this time of night, you'll never get to sleep."

That was Julie's favorite go-to comfort food, pickles dipped in hot caramel. And after the weekend she'd had, that was the least she could allow herself for managing to survive.

"Fine. The caramel is in the fridge," Hannah said as she poured them both a cup of steaming chocolate milk. "Just do me a favor. Wait until I'm done with this before you start in on that gross concoction. I don't think I can watch it tonight."

"Deal."

Hannah sat down next to her. They were silent for a few moments, both listening to the sound of the clock ticking and the normal creaks and groans of the old house. "Would you like a cookie?"

Julie smiled over the rim of her mug. "That would be almost as good as pickles and caramel."

Hannah pushed a sealed container toward Julie. Sweet molasses spice cookies were nestled inside.

"Delicious," Julie said around the first mouthful. She swallowed and took another bite. She hadn't realized how hungry almost getting killed a few times in one night could make a person.

"This hasn't exactly turned out to be the quiet town we

thought we were moving to, has it?" Hannah said.

"Not even close." Julie had long since decided that Straussberg was anything but quiet. That wasn't necessarily a bad thing. She was an action junkie. She thrived on the unknown. The town was definitely starting to grow on her.

"You've got that gleam in your eyes again." Hannah raised an eyebrow in her direction. She knew Julie so well.

"It's nothing. Just thinking about this town."

"You're not thinking of leaving, are you?" Hannah asked. Julie heard the unmistakable worry in her friend's voice. She knew Hannah had grown fond of the new job and the people of Straussberg.

Julie scoffed. "Are you kidding? And miss the all the excitement?" She raised her mug for a toast. "Here's to our next adventure at the Quilt Haus Inn."

Hannah smiled and raised her mug to clink against Julie's. "Here, here."

And for the first time in days, Julie saw Hannah relax.

EIGHTEEN

At ten o'clock the next morning, the remaining guests gathered to check out and say their goodbyes. Even Liam had shown up, though he wasn't leaving.

"I had such a wonderful time," Joyce gushed, pulling Julie in for a quick hug. "I haven't had that much excitement in years!"

"I can't wait to come back for the murder mystery weekend next year," Sadie said. Not one to be left out, she snatched a hug as well. "Though I don't know how you'll possibly top this one."

"We've got to start saving this very instant," Joyce said.

"Immediately," Sadie confirmed.

Julie didn't have the heart to tell them there wouldn't be a murder mystery weekend next year—or *any* year in the foreseeable future if *she* had anything to say about it.

"Most fun I've had in years." Kenneth grinned, looking far more relaxed than he had when he arrived. "We'll definitely be back next year."

Julie merely smiled.

Everyone grabbed their bags and headed for the door, smiling and waving with promises to return.

Julie shut the door behind them and turned to face Liam.

"Don't look at me," he said. "I may not leave until next year. This place is very inspiring."

Julie rolled her eyes.

Liam chuckled and headed up to his room.

Still keyed up, Julie felt like she needed to do something, fix something, find something, investigate something. The weekend had been nonstop, and her mind and body were still in high gear.

Instead, she channeled her nervous energy and crossed to the registration desk to check on the new guests that were due to arrive later in the day. She had a young couple coming in from Denver and a pair of sisters coming in from Oklahoma. Nice and normal—one would hope.

The bell over the door rang. She looked up to see a man enter. He was small, on the mousey side, and balding with a thick ring of black hair around his head. His glasses were reminiscent of Buddy Holly's, though somehow not as cool. He carried a briefcase in one hand while the other twisted nervously.

"Can I help you?" Julie asked, straightening as he cautiously approached.

"I certainly hope so." His voice was surprisingly steady and confident. "I'm Aston Cooper. I've come to examine your journal."

"Oh, my. Yes," Aston said.

Julie looked to Daniel, who continued to smile with satisfaction. She had called him to join her for the big moment. He deserved it. Also, she was wary of being alone with a stranger and the Civil War book.

Aston delicately turned the page of the journal and ran his magnifying glass down the page, examining every detail. "Yes, yes, yes. Uh-huh." He continued to mutter to himself as he inspected the next page.

"Well?" Julie prompted.

Aston sat back in his seat and smiled at them both. "You

have yourself a fine treasure here. A fine treasure."

"And?" Daniel asked. One would think the book actually belonged to him considering how excited he was.

"The time frame is definitely correct. Clemens joined the Civil War in 1861, but he only stayed for two weeks. Their company was away from the war and didn't get any attention from the commanding officers. This lack of direction was their downfall. The men disbanded and went their separate ways." Aston opened his tablet and found the file he was looking for. "This is a copy of Samuel Clemens's signature as both himself and Mark Twain. Now look here." He opened the book and pointed out all the similarities in the script. The more he talked, the more excited Julie became until she rivaled Daniel in her enthusiasm.

"The fact that this is one of the first rule books from baseball makes it very valuable in and of itself," Aston continued. "But given that it was used as a journal by someone famous increases its worth exponentially. Add in the fact that there are notes which could be the start of a great American novel, and you have a priceless treasure on your hands."

"Told you!" Daniel crossed his arms and smiled at Julie, looking more than pleased with himself. "And you *cannot* put that in the school auction."

Aston's expression morphed from happy to horrified. "Oh my. No. This treasure belongs in a museum."

"And I know just the place for it." Daniel's eyes sparkled.

Aston ignored Daniel's comment. "In fact, I'm willing to offer you a great deal of money for it." He quickly wrote out a check and pushed it across the desk toward Julie.

She didn't pick it up. Instead she stared at it and all the zeroes. Money like that would keep the Quilt Haus Inn in the black for a long, long time.

"I think you might have misunderstood, Mr. Cooper. The book doesn't belong to me. It belongs to the inn's owner, and she's not here right now."

His face fell, but he recovered fast. "Would you be willing to contact her with my offer?"

"Of course. I'll try and reach her this afternoon," she said. "But I can't make any promises." If there was one thing about Millie, she was anything but predictable.

Aston stood and handed her a business card. Then he picked up the check and put it away. "You have my number, but just in case, I'm staying at the River Bluff Hotel. Let me know when you hear from her."

Julie nodded. "I will."

She walked Aston to the front door, thanking him for his time and for coming all the way to Straussberg.

After he was gone, Daniel really let his excitement show. "Can you believe it?" he asked, jumping up to do a little victory dance.

Julie grinned. What she couldn't quite believe was how adorable Daniel was when his guard was down completely. "It is pretty amazing."

Millie called Julie back shortly after the Denver couple checked in. As Julie suspected, the eccentric owner wasn't interested in money. She was more worried about preserving the heritage and well-being of their small Missouri town. She wanted to keep the journal in Straussberg. She agreed to donate it to Daniel's new museum on the condition that he always keep it and make it a special exhibit.

"Absolutely," Daniel said. His museum was dedicated to

the steamboat wreckage he had unearthed the previous year, but he could definitely find room for a priceless treasure like the book. "Let's see, we'll need a tighter security system and a special case." He paced the floor, muttering to himself about making a video with images of the pages so that visitors could see the notes without actually touching the book. It was a good thing he came from money; otherwise, his elaborate project would be dead in the water before it even got started.

Aston took the news fairly well, considering his strong personal interest in the book. But Julie had a feeling he'd be contacting Millie every six months to see if anything had changed.

"Do you realize how many new tourists this will bring to our community?" Daniel asked.

"I hope it brings better people than Gregory Wilson to Straussberg," Julie answered.

"It'll mean so much to the town."

Julie nodded in agreement, although she doubted that half the citizens under the age of thirty would understand its worth. "That's all well and good," she said, locking the book inside the safe, where it would remain until Daniel had a place for it. "But there's still an auction, and I have nothing to donate."

"I thought you found a couple of books in the cellar."

"I did, but I'm not sure that's what I want to donate."

He crossed his arms across his broad chest and shot her a look that said he knew what was coming next. "I've already told you how I feel about you pulling anything else out of that basement. Who knows what can of worms you might open next?"

"I don't plan on going to the basement."

"Oh, really? Then why do you have that gleam in your eye?"

She grinned. "Come up to the attic with me and find out.

I thought I might look *there* for a new donation."

He threw his head back and laughed. "I think you only want me along to kill the spiders."

"Busted."

"All right. I'll go with you on one condition."

"What's that?"

"Whatever we discover up there, we tell *no one* until it's out of the mansion and in the school's possession," he said. "Certainly no one from the local newspaper."

"It's a deal," Julie said. Then she led the way up the Quilt Haus Inn stairs.

Millie's Coffee Cup Cozy

Specifications

Finished Cozy Size: 10½" x 3½"
  (including binding)

Skill Level: Beginner

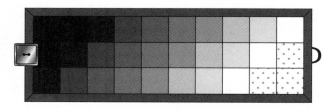

Millie's Coffee Cup Cozy
Placement Diagram 10½" x 3½" (including binding)

Cutting

From 10 (5") Squares Gradated Light-to-Dark Solids:
Cut 3 (1½") A squares from each fabric.

From Coordinating Dark Solid Fat Quarter:
Cut 2 (2¼" x 21") strips for binding.

Assembly

1. Join the A squares in 10 rows of three squares each (Figure 1); press seams in opposite directions from row to row.

Figure 1

2. Join the rows to complete the top; press.

3. Layer a 5½" x 12½" backing rectangle, right side down; a 5½" x 12½" batting rectangle; and the cozy top, right side up; baste or pin to hold. Quilt as desired. Trim edges even with the top.

4. Join binding strips on short ends with a diagonal seam; trim seam to ¼" and press open.

5. Fold binding strip in half with wrong sides together along length; press.

6. Sew binding to cozy top, matching raw edges, mitering corners and overlapping ends.

7. Fold binding to the back side and stitch in place.

8. Sew a 1" button to the top centered on the left end of the cozy referring to the Placement Diagram.

9. Make a loop with a 3" length of elastic cord; knot the ends. Hand-stitch the knotted end to the back centered on the right end of the cozy. Add a drop of fabric glue to the knot if desired.

10. Wrap the cozy around a coffee cup and place the loop over the button to use.

HELPFUL HINTS
• Use a ¼"-wide seam allowance for all seams and stitch right sides together.

• For more detailed help with quilting techniques, go to QuiltersWorld.com and choose Quilting Basics under Quilt Essentials, or consult a complete quilting guide. Your local library may have several on hand that you can review before purchasing one.

A VINEYARD QUILT MYSTERY™

DON'T MISS THE NEXT VINEYARD QUILT MYSTERY

Log on to AnniesCraftStore.com to preview and purchase additional books in the series now!

Log on to
AnniesCraftStore.com/Vineyard
to sign up for new release alerts,
AND you'll get a special coupon
for **15% OFF** your next purchase
with Annie's!